Lorne Oliver

The
Chimes

Also by Lorne Oliver

Sgt. Reid Series
Red Island
Red Serge

The Alcrest Mysteries
The Cistern
The Menu
The Pass

The Alcrest Gastropub
Cookbook

THE CHIMES

Copyright © 2017 by Lorne Oliver

ISBN 978-0-9940309-2-4

Cover design: Chelsea Barnes at CJPB Designs

Author Notes

The voices keep talking. In 2013 I started writing about the gang at the Alcrest and they haven't stopped talking since. I'm not complaining. I've come to enjoy their constant chatter in the Middleton section of my brain. They've all developed and grown as I try getting their stories out as fast as I can. Any mistakes made are clearly my own.

My family suffers. They suffer the fact that my mind is taken up by these other people. They suffer me suddenly talking about lives they know little about. They deal with me talking about crimes and ideas. They are my support. Brandi, Jordann, Wylie you inspire and encourage me every day.

Thank you to Elizabeth Frances for being who you are. Thank you Sandra, Mitch and Linda for all of your hard work.

Samara, welcome to the Alcrest.

To everyone else, if this is your first time you are welcome to come into the Alcrest Gastropub for a bite to eat any time. If you have returned again your spot is waiting for you.

Chimes

A bell or a metal bar or tube that produces a melodious series of ringing sounds when struck.

Wind-Chimes

A decorative set of glass, metal, wood or other pieces to make a relaxing sound in the breeze.

Prologue

Before I slide my souvenir ticket off the counter the clerk has already gone to the person behind me as if I'm not even there. I'm a nuisance which must be brushed aside. Some would call it rude. I can live with it. She'll know me soon enough, or what I can do.

The clerk says, "Tonight's the night Chrys," eager to get on with someone more important.

The customer is pretty. Not really my type. Her skin is too dark and she's too full of life. "Yeah, I need 7 tickets. Hi."

The last is said to me accompanied by a smile of full lips. I nod and slip away. She'll forget me in seconds. She probably forgot me before I even nodded. I'll get on the bus with all the others, sit in my seat like I've done a dozen times before and no one will really see me. Someone will even try to sit on me. "Oops, sorry. Didn't see you there." They won't remember seeing me by the start of the tour and the man who almost sat on me will forget by the time he takes his seat and places his daughter on his lap, but they'll all remember what they see.

Near the end of the tour the bus will come to a spot in the woods of Leigh Park where I've hung a silent wind-chime. It might still be dripping. Drip. At first they won't believe what they see. Their brains will say it's not real. It's part of the ghost tour, that's all. Then one will scream. I'm guessing the woman with the three children will be the first. She keeps asking her husband if their kids are old enough for the scary tour. "They're just stories," he says. When they see what I have waiting for them his mouth will gape open with no explanations to spew. A swarm of flies would be able to land on his tongue. Others will follow the first scream as they realize it's not part of the tour. Some will hide their faces. Some will have to look between their fingers like they would at a scary movie. How many camera phones will be broken out?

I bet the one named Chrys won't scream at all. Will she be afraid or turned on? I'd like to pick her brain afterward if I could.

They are all my actors. I'm the director of this play. I'll be sitting in the dark wings unseen and unnoticed like I'm on the edge of the stage listening to them scream, as I try to hide my Joker's smile and hard cock. Still they won't notice me. They'll be sitting with a killer looking at his artwork and won't have a clue.

I've been hiding too long. It's time to make a scene. Action!

Chapter 1

"This is gonna be fun," Chrys Alcrest did a double step. Her Steve Madden ankle boots clicked on the faux-cobblestones outside the tourist center.

Spencer Alcrest shoved his hands in the pockets of his cashmere coat. The beauty of living on the west coast of Canada was that snow and winter didn't last long. That didn't mean it wasn't still chilly at night. "How much is this costing me?"

"Nothing. I'm paying for it." Chrys bounced and smiled bright.

His eyebrows popped up. "You're paying for the whole crew to go on this bus thing? Since when do you have money?" His foster-sister had been putting in less hours at the restaurant with their family name on it, but was always there to get free food. He was starting to understand why. She had always had her own little secrets.

Her smile disappeared and somehow her pillowy lips looked thin. "You're a downer."

"I can leave if you want."

"No you can't." Chrys stepped in front of him to block his path. The two of them considered each other blood-related siblings, however over the past few months she had started to wonder why. He was becoming a real tyrant asshole both in the restaurant and at home. "I'm paying for this. I teach at the dance studio, I've been putting in hours for Hoyt at the locksmiths and," Chrys stopped herself before she said anything else to her brother. She realized half of the staff from The Alcrest Gastropub was right there pretending not to listen. She didn't need everyone knowing what other side job she had and wasn't ready yet to tell her brother. It was going to piss him off and that wasn't a fight she wanted to have out in public. "I have more money than you know, Spence. Leave it at that. Fuck."

"Then why don't you pay some of the bills at home?" He turned away from her and joined the others, still with his hands in his pockets.

It was almost midnight on a chilly April night. Chrys had convinced most of the restaurant's evening shift to come to this. All of the servers came – well, there had only been two on, Hanni and Wylie. Wylie seemed excited about the ride and even called his fiancée to come down. Chrys was paying for her too. Hanni looked less enthusiastic. Chrys really didn't want the slooty bitch there, but she had been working and couldn't exclude her. All of the cooks came. Gordie was off somewhere probably smoking something of a questionable nature, Ranger and Mallory were by the door of the bus with their shoulders slouched not talking to each other or anyone else for that matter.

There were other people hanging around waiting for the tour. A few parents tried to reign in their children who were excited to still be up so late. A man carried a little girl wrapped in a Disney Princess blanket. The girl struggled to keep her eyes open. A couple stood by the tourist center wall cuddling to stay warm. Most of the crowd was from out of town. A few looked like they were from different countries.

After a minute of deep breaths to calm herself Chrys tucked her long chestnut hair, in the dim light it looked black, inside her jacket and stepped beside her brother. "Why didn't Jessie come?"

"She was tired." Spencer's voice was absent and quick as if it was just a stock response.

Chrys stomped her feet on the ground to get some feeling in them. "What's going on with you two?"

Spencer looked up, but didn't look at his sister. His eyes caught Hanni's gaze. "Nothing," he said. Another stock response.

"Come on." Chrys was fearless and often seemed to lack that little voice that said, shut up. "I don't know when she last stayed over. I may not be a fan of hers, but I thought you guys were something. What's going on?"

"Nothing, I said. Why don't you talk about your own life and leave mine alone?" Spencer and Jessie, the front-of-house manager at the restaurant, had been an item for 4 years, however almost a year ago their relationship started to get extremely strained. Strained enough that for the past few weeks they only spoke during work hours. Spencer didn't know what would happen. He was pretty sure things had gone too far for anything to be fixed.

"You are such a dick." Chrys wrapped her arms around her body.

The Midnight in Middleton Ghost Tour had been a draw for locals and tourists for almost 10 years. The motor coach (the sides of which were painted with a woman in a ghostly white gown walking on a stormy shore) left the tourist center at midnight and zig-zagged through the streets as a guide told the haunting stories of the city's past. For some it could get spooky, but it was all in good fun. Near the end of the tour the driver pretended the bus broke down in the wooded park that everyone knew was haunted. The driver would flick the lights, pump the breaks and pretend the engine shut down to scare the crap out of everyone. Chrys and her friends tried camping out there for one night and couldn't do it. She had been on the ride three times in the last week and it frightened her every time. The ghost stories of Leigh Park were well known amongst the kids of Middleton. After they would have their laugh the driver would start up the coach and it would return to the tourist center where everyone went on their way to have nightmares. It was in all the tourist guides and had even been mentioned in a few magazines as 1 of the top 10 things to do in Middleton.

The coach tour season had just started with some new stories added onto the tour. That was why she made everyone come out.

Chrys took a breath and let it out slow. She stepped beside a man with a round belly pushing out his City of Middleton jacket and put her shoulders back, chest out, chin up. "Could I have everyone's attention please? My name is Chrys and I'll be tonight's guide into the ghostly stories of Middleton's past. As you come on board please show me your souvenir ticket and take a seat. You will see a few reserved seats for a group from The Alcrest Gastropub in the front, so please don't sit there unless you are part of that group. And nobody sit directly behind the bus driver unless you want me to sit in your lap. Okay?"

There was a snort from the man holding the little girl. He got an elbow from his wife because of it.

This was just the first of the jobs Chrys had been doing which she didn't tell her big brother about. She avoided his gaze as he climbed onboard.

After the last guest climbed into the bus Chrys followed. Her eyes fell on the seat behind the one saved for her. Hanni sat next to the window and Spencer right beside her. The two women didn't get along, even though they had each saved the others life, and that wasn't about to change. Chrys didn't like the way she was around her brother. Hanni served at the restaurant and would flirt with anyone to get bigger tips. Her push-up bras and tight skirts barely hid anything. She was shameless about it. Chrys was sure the woman was high on something most of the time too. Chrys really didn't like her sitting with her brother.

Hanni liked doing what she could to make Spencer, the chef and owner of The Alcrest Gastropub, as nervous and uncomfortable as she could. The fact that it pissed off his foster-sister was a bonus. Even if it meant grabbing his ass in front of his girlfriend who was also her direct supervisor. She looked up at Chrys with a perfect "resting-bitch-face"

Chrys shook her head. She didn't get her brother lately. It was his life though. If he wanted to ruin it with slut petri dishes then that was up to him. She put a microphone headset over her right ear, the lobe of which was slightly deformed, and flicked the on switch. "Can everyone hear me?" There were some responses. "You sir, in the back, can you hear me?"

"Yes, I…I can."

"Okay, welcome everyone to the Midnight in Middleton Ghost Tour. As I said outside, my name is Chrys. Your driver tonight is Jerry. Say hi, Jerry." She waited for him to wave. "Tonight we are going to tour the city as I tell you tales of ghosts, spirits, strange occurrences, dastardly crimes and cases of murder. The City of Middleton has a long and colourful past. Some of these stories are from before Canada was even a country, some are from the last century and a couple are as recent as last year's news headlines."

Spencer's head popped up. His aquamarine eyes blasted fire at his Aboriginal foster-sister. If she was talking about what he thought she was talking about… He was going to kill her.

Chrys wouldn't look down at him. As the bus started to move again she was still standing holding onto a metal bar. Even though she couldn't see all the way to the back she looked there. She felt her brother's eyes burning into her. "I will tell you things that may shock you. I will tell you things which will frighten you. Please note, that every story I do tell you is absolutely, one hundred percent true, no matter how outlandish it may seem. Sit back as we go into the world of the macabre."

Spencer had gone on the tour a couple of years ago with Jessie. It always started at the Aeronautics Museum just down the street. Chrys talked about the World War Two pilot whose plane was inside and how he had been spotted walking the floors. Also about Wendell the janitor who died there from a heart attack and still could be heard sweeping the foyer. The moment she was done telling the stories she sat down and the bus continued.

14

Spencer sat with his arms crossed in front of him. He had things he could be doing instead of sitting on a bus listening to his sister tell ghost stories. The restaurant wasn't in a good place. They had been losing customers over the past year which meant bills weren't being paid. As far as cutting corners to pay those bills, he didn't know what else he could do. He loved the fact that he made a new menu all the time depending on what was at the butchers, farmer's or fish markets, however if customers didn't want what he had planned all of that went to waste. He didn't want to be one of those places with the same menu day after day, but he was becoming just that. He kept items on the menu lately because they sold. That was never the plan. He wondered if his dad went through the same thing all the years that he ran The Alcrest. Too bad he was gone. Back then it was a pub and the food was second to the beer and booze. Spencer also wondered if his dad was as angry as he had become. He remembered his father yelling, but for him it was becoming overwhelming. Being on this ride wasn't helping.

Spencer felt Hanni's French-tipped nails running up and down his thigh. Even that wasn't helping with his mood. She had a way of getting him excited to the point of feeling uncomfortable like he should either run or give in. Only lately it wasn't uncomfortable that he was feeling. Not with her anyway.

As the bus slowed Chrys stood and turned around. She wrapped an arm around the metal support pole before glaring down at her brother for a few seconds. She looked to the back of the bus again. "Okay everyone, the area of town we are coming into was, at the turn of the twentieth century, China Town. It is of course now known as Old

China Town. So creative right? In 1908 opium became illegal and as the story goes the opium and gambling dens moved to tunnels beneath Old China Town. The story is that …" as she spoke her eyes continued to drop down to her brother. Hanni was now whispering in his ear. He smiled and nodded. What did that mean? What poison was she spreading? "… As the myth goes that is why this street is called Butcher's Alley. The truth is probably that an important politician at the time was John H. Butcher, so the alley is most likely named after him. We are now going to head to a brand new addition to the tour and this one is no myth."

As soon as Chrys was down in her seat she turned off the microphone and twisted around the back to see what was happening in her brother's lap. Even in the dim light she saw the blond woman was pressed up against Spencer. "What the hell are you doing?"

"What?" Spencer snapped.

Hanni took the moment to put her hand on-top of his thigh and gave it a squeeze. "Leave us alone, Chrys."

"Do you mind? I'm talking to my brother." Chrys stared at her until she turned to the window with a flourish of her long hair. Chrys noticed Hanni's hand never left her brother's leg. "Cut it out, Spence."

His arms were still crossed over his chest. "Don't tell me what to do, Chrys. And where are we going?"

"A new spot on the tour."

"Which is?"

"Wait and see." Chrys turned back to face the front. She didn't have quite the flourish in her locks. Hearing Hanni and Spencer laugh behind her made her entire body shiver.

Spencer knew exactly where they were going. They had already crossed into the part of Middleton called Fontana. It was mainly a residential area with a lot of smaller, family owned businesses on certain streets and some right out of people's homes. Pretty soon they'd be heading up Pearson Street. He was pretty sure the address they were going to was 3231 Pearson between Gillies and Scoble. He was going to throttle his sister.

Hanni screeched. She leapt away from the window almost climbing over Spencer's lap. Mallory screamed. Chrys let out a little yelp. Others in the bus yelled and flinched away from the left side windows.

It took half a block before Chrys had her microphone back on. She chose not to stand. Her knees felt week. "Everyone have a little scare there? That has become the latest Middleton Mystery. Two or three nights a week people have reported seeing a mysterious clown on random street corners." Tonight he had been standing on the opposite side of the street almost staring at the bus as it went by. He was dressed in a baggy suit of yellow, blue and white with large red puff-balls down the front. His face was all white except a painted on smile, red nose and blue around the eyes. In the street light his wild hair looked orange. For Chrys the creepiest part was that the three balloons he held in one hand didn't move in the wind. She continued, "Some of the younger crowd have now made it a game trying to find the clown so they can get their picture with him. Nobody knows why he's out there or where he came from. He just appears on street corners."

"Who the hell would do that?" Hanni was much louder than she needed to be. Her entire body trembled. She had always been terrified of clowns. She pulled a flask out from inside her coat.

"There are a few theories floating around social media," Chrys said over the loud speakers. "Lunatic escaped from a mental hospital? A college student trying to prove something? A demonic creature wanting to eat our souls? Some have even said that it may be more than one person and that is why he's so hard to catch on film."

"Here we are at our next stop." Chrys quickly got to her feet. "A favorite meal spot in Middleton, The Alcrest Gastropub, has now become more well-known because of a brutal murder just last year. The headless body of one of their very own cooks was burned to a crisp in the restaurants very own oven just last year."

The only thing that had changed to the front of the faded brick building since back in the day when it was a pub was the large bay window with the restaurant's name etched on it. It had to be replaced last summer. Beside the front door, imbedded in the wall, was a polished rectangle of black granite with Alcrest carved in script. Above that was a protruding white lion head. The lion was picked as the family crest because nobody knew what the actual crest was. This lion was either snarling or smiling depending on how you looked at it.

Spencer thought about standing up and demanding to be let out. He and his sister shared the apartment above the restaurant. If his truck wasn't half-way across the city at the tourist center he would have done it. Instead he stared up at her hoping she could read his mind. There was no question of whether his lips were a snarl or smile.

Chrys refused to look down at him. "Some of the employees at The Alcrest swear they have felt or seen a

18

ghostly presence late at night." Everyone in the first few seats looked at each other. The truthful parts of this tour were questionable. "I highly recommend the pasta dishes. Now, sit back and relax as we head to more places of horror." She sat down as the bus started again.

Spencer leaned around the seat. "What the hell was that?"

"Advertising."

"By telling people about the body in the oven? You missed where we found her head. How about that we have brand new ovens? This is going to drive people away, not bring them in. Not to mention disrespectful to -"

"I never said her name and you underestimate the power of a spooky story, dear brother. People love a spooky story and they'll come to the restaurant because of it. What if they want to see a ghost?"

"They'll be disappointed." This was ridiculous. Why was his sister always doing crazy things? Why was he always picking up the pieces? Spencer couldn't hold his thoughts any longer. "From now on keep your hands and schemes away from my restaurant. I'm barely surviving as it is."

Chrys flinched. "I thought it was The Alcrest restaurant, not Spencer Alcrest's restaurant?"

"This is all I've got, Chrys."

"And what do I have, Spence? This is my future too you know. I'm trying to help." Her face burned. Her eyes swelled.

Spencer felt his staff watching and listening. He was the leader. He couldn't let his sister control him. What he should have said next was that Chrys had her dancing and modelling and that she was going to go places. She didn't need the restaurant. That was what he should have said. What he actually said was, "You're not an Alcrest."

Chrys stared at his eyes. When she was three her mother didn't pick her up from daycare. She disappeared. She dropped her child off in the morning and then was gone. Chrys went to live with the Alcrest family. She became part of it. She was an Alcrest. She thought her foster-brother felt the same. Chrys flicked on her microphone. "FUCK YOU!" Her words came out of every speaker inside the bus. She turned back to face the front and slumped down in her seat.

She didn't want to cry and give him the satisfaction. Screw Spencer. Screw his stupid restaurant. Screw the blond slut sitting with him. Chrys didn't know what was going on with her brother. He'd never said anything like that to her before. They always treated each other like a real brother and sister would. They fought now and then, but were always there for each other. Chrys didn't know if it was like that anymore. She wiped a tear from her cheek.

She knew people had always looked at them with strange expressions when the family was out. Here was this white Caucasian family with a little girl the colour of creamy coffee. Three blond people and a girl with chestnut hair, right. She knew people always saw her as a special case. The white family that saved the little Native girl. She didn't think her own brother thought that way. She let the tears run down her face.

Spencer stared at the back of her head. How dare she do this? She never thought about what she was doing. He ignored Hanni's hand gripping his inner thigh. He did take her flask though and took a drink.

20

As Chrys stood and faced the back of the tour bus she focused on the black shadows of people farther back. The light which spotlighted her showed a glistening on her cheeks. Her voice cracked as she started to speak. She had to pause, clear her throat and start over. "Excuse me. In 1922, Leigh Park was the site for one of Middleton's most infamous murder mysteries. Even today, almost one hundred years later, the police still consider it an open case. It's the case of the Twin Boys of Leigh Park."

The bus drove below a wrought iron archway with, Leigh Park, spelled out above the road. It was a provincial park in the North-west corner of the city almost completely surrounded by water – the Pacific on one side and Winchester Bay on two others. To protect the park from the changing tide the Middleton Seawall had been built around the outer edges almost around the same time as the twin boys were found. Hundreds, if not thousands, of people visited the park every day to run, walk or bike. Most of the 1000-acre park was made of dense West Coast rainforest that was hundreds of years old. Some of the oldest were around 700 years old including the Cave Tree which people could drive their cars through. Cedars, maples, spruce and other trees made the forest look amazing and filled your nostrils with brilliant smells. Every once in a while a wind storm ravaged parts of the park, but the resilience of nature always came back. There were hiking trails, beaches, a small par 3 golf course and an aquarium with fish of the Pacific Ocean. The Alcrest family had gone there every Canada Day since Chrys and Spencer were kids to listen to live music and watch the fireworks get set off in the bay. The aquarium was still one of Chrys' favorite places to spend a day. She had been taken to different parts of the park many times on dates.

"It was a cold, rainy August day when one of the men working on the Seawall walked into the woods to do his business." Chrys paused for the usual chuckle. "It was then that he came upon the most terrifying thing he had ever seen in his entire life. Two boys, almost identical, lay beneath a giant redwood holding hands. Their bodies were half covered by dead leaves and branches in an attempt to hide them." The bus continued driving into the towering forest as she spoke. "It was reported later that one had been beaten with a rock and the other stabbed in the heart. They were dressed in their Sunday best. Each one's hair was cut nicely, nails trimmed. Except for the dirt and blood on their clothes they were dressed like high society children, yet nobody ever came forward with their identities. Their pictures and descriptions were printed in every newspaper from Anchorage down to Seattle and as Far East as Calgary, yet nobody ever came forward to claim their bodies and perhaps put a light onto what happened to these poor children. They became known as the Leigh Twins and in fact were buried together beneath a marker labeling them as such. Their killer was also never identified."

The bus lurched to one side. The light focused on Chrys flickered off and on. The thin road they were on had towering dark trees on either side. Looking out the windows the tour customers only saw black and shadow. Someone near the back gasped.

Chrys let out a nervous laugh. "It looks like even the driver is getting afraid. Everything alright, Jerry?"

He gave her a nod.

Chrys cleared her throat playing her nervous host routine very well. "There were no other clues besides the boy's bodies and soon the mystery was forgotten as it faded into myth. Night hikers in the woods have reported many strange things such as children's laughter in the wind and dancing lights amongst the trees. Over the past fifty years night hikers had reported the ghostly-white image of two boys walking through the forest holding hands. Whatever happened to their killer? Why did this happen to them? Why didn't anyone ever come forward to give a name to the boys? Will the Leigh Twins ever get to rest?" She glared down at Hanni. "Was the killer the clown that now wanders our streets?"

Hanni glowered up at Chrys. She was having fun on this trip. She liked pissing off the dark haired woman with her hand on Spencer's leg. She was whispering things in his ear that obviously made him uncomfortable. She had been playing this game for a couple years and was getting close to the end. She was never satisfied once she got what she wanted though and wasn't sure how this was going to go.

The bus braked then lurched forward. Chrys was ready for it. One hand held onto the metal pole as she lunged toward the dashboard then pulled herself back. The bus reeled from one side to the other as if something was terribly wrong. It was all part of the ride. They were going to pretend the bus broke down in a couple minutes. Jerry would get off to see if he could fix it and all the passengers would sit in the dark waiting to see if he would return. After a few minutes people usually began to question where he was. Meanwhile outside Jerry would play the sound of children laughing. A couple more minutes and he'd run on the bus startling everyone.

23

The light on Chrys flashed off and on again. The bus bounced as Jerry aimed for every rock and pothole. Hanni let out a little noise. Fucking wimp, Chrys thought. Jerry played with the headlights so they were flickering. He'd come to a stop right on the corner. The bus started the turn. He turned the headlights off. His foot pushed the brake pedal hard. He turned the lights back on.

Hanni let out a banshee wail. Spencer flinched back from her.

"Hanni?" Spencer stared at the woman beside him. Her nails dug into his leg. Her blue eyes were wide as saucers. "Hanni, what is it?"

Another scream erupted from near the back of the bus. Spencer looked to the back. Jerry swore. Mallory screamed. Chrys turned and looked out the windshield. She suddenly stumbled back away from it. Her heels caught on the floor. Spencer reached out and caught her.

Six items swayed together below the branch of a maple. The outer five banged against the middle item. Was there a sound? Leaves fluttered around them. Blood fell. Drip. Two forearms swayed, one hand was hanging down and the other was tied to the tree limb by the middle finger with the others curled down, knocking against hanging feet. That wasn't what made Hanni scream. It was the face in the middle. Some of the hair was up tied by a string to the branch above like a sick pony-tail. As it turned in the breeze white eyes stared at the bus.

This was not part of the tour.

Chapter 2

"Who are you?"

"Chrys Alcrest. I mean Wanderingspirit. Chrysanthemum Wanderingspirit." She glared at her brother. If he didn't want her to be part of the family then she'd use her original last name. Screw him.

"You don't know your own name?"

Chrys blinked. "Who are you?"

The woman in front of her rolled her eyes. She wore rectangle glasses which didn't hide the bags beneath her eyes, a leather jacket over a black top and charcoal pants. She stood straight, no slouching. "Detective Washburn, Middleton Police, Homicide." Her voice had that commanding tone that said she was tired of Chrys already.

"Where's Constable Wright?"

After seeing the body parts Jerry had backed the bus up far enough that they could no longer see the hanging pieces before calling the police. Children were crying. Someone kept repeating "Oh my God" over and over. Chrys was tempted to get off the bus and go take a look. Just a little peak to see if she could identify the dead person or find anything left. She had the mystery fever. As soon as the police were called Jerry backed the bus up even more.

Almost everyone was gone now and were being replaced by a growing crowd of onlookers that reminded Spencer of a growing herd of zombies against a fence in a television show he liked. After the detective spoke to all of the passengers the bus took them back to the tourist center and their vehicles. The Alcrest's were told to stay.

"He transferred out of homicide. Look, I've been told about you and your brother and all your antics. I know you put your noses in where they don't belong. I also know you've almost had those noses cut off more than once. That can't happen anymore. I don't need any damn vigilantes getting in my way."

Spencer put his hands up. "I want none of this. I've got my own stuff to deal with. I was just along for the ride."

Chrys huffed and kicked at the wet grass.

The police crime lab had large spotlights up on tripods. Police officers came and went toward where the macabre tree ornament was, always looking to the detective for direction. There were cars with flashing lights all along the road and yellow tape strung up between trees.

"Have you been drinking, Mr. Alcrest?"

He rubbed his eyes. "You finish a day's work and your sister takes you on this bullshit bus tour, so yeah, I had a swig or two. She's the one you have to worry about."

She's the one you have to worry about? What the hell was that supposed to mean? Chrys looked at her brother with a "thanks for throwing me under the bus, bro" look. He turned away. Since when did he refer to her like that? She's the one!

26

Detective Washburn put her attention on Chrys. "Are you staying out of this?" The police detective wasn't stunning, but her demeanor made you take a second look. She carried herself well. That and legs up to her neck.

Chrys was both – confident and attractive. Both were attributes that could usually draw people to her. Of course they could also get her in a world of trouble. She had that girl-next-door thing going for her which people either loved or hated. She dropped her eyes like a little girl being scolded. The detective didn't seem to get that she was supposed to like Chrys.

"You haven't answered me yet."

Chrys looked up and snarled. "I won't do anything. Okay?"

"Hey," Detective Washburn snapped as she stepped toward her. "From what I've been told you two have almost been killed yourselves more than once." She looked at Spencer. "You were tortured, weren't you?" She turned back to Chrys. "Stay out of this. It's your only warning." She slipped an elastic band from her wrist and tied her straight blond hair back. One strand fell down alongside her face. "Didn't I see somewhere that you two have ties to the Irish mob?"

Chrys puffed air out. "Not even."

"We know Liam O'Donnell," Spencer said after stepping in front of his foster-sister. He was pretty sure the detective knew everything about them. There was no point in trying to lie and he really needed his sister to shut up. "I wouldn't say we have ties to the mob or anything. He knew my father back in the day. That's it."

He knew MY father, Spencer hated admitting that his dad knew the man who ran the loading docks and was suspected of every crime out there. In the past year the siblings have had to depend on the killer for way too much. Hopefully that was over with. Why was the detective asking about it? Did this have something to do with O'Donnell?

"Sounds like ties to me. Stay away from all of this. If you don't, I'll put you in jail and won't lose any sleep over it." With that she turned and walked toward the bright lights.

Spencer walked past his sister heading toward the police barrier and the park entrance beyond that.

"What's your problem?" Chrys quickened her pace to be beside him.

He pushed his hands in his coat pockets. His blond spikes glistened with the early morning dew. "Some of us have to work in a couple hours."

"What's that supposed to mean?"

"Jesus! It means I work early in the morning, Chrys." Beyond all the police vehicles waited Spencer's blue 4x4. As they got close the driver's door opened and Hanni slipped out.

Chrys froze.

Spencer looked back at her. She was still his sister no matter what he said. "You coming?"

Without saying a word Chrys tried to show her anger and disgust in one facial expression. "I'd rather walk. What is she doing here?"

"Come on, it's three in the morning. I want a little sleep." Spencer looked at her face and wondered what was up with her scrunched up nose and snarling lip. He could see there was anger in her eyes, but the rest of her looked like she was having cramps. After a second he decided he didn't care. "You do whatever you want. We're going home."

"Oh, *WE* are going home. Since when did you and Hanni become a we?" Chrys caught Hanni's "wicked witch" scowl as she handed Spencer the keys and walked around to the passenger side.

Spencer opened the driver's door before responding. "What the hell are you talking about? What, Hanni? She brought US my truck so you and I can go home. I'm dropping her off on the way. You coming or not?"

Thousands of people used Leigh Park every day, but that didn't mean you wanted to be there in the middle of the night. Even with the large police presence. You never knew who or what would be out there hiding in the trees. Plus their apartment was on the far side of the city. Chrys was in shape and could easily walk the distance, however the want to do it wasn't there. She gave up and stomped to the truck. "Fine, but since you've been drinking I'm driving."

"I haven't had that much, Chrys."

"Bullshit!" She snatched the keys out of his hand. "You were three sheets to the wind before we left the restaurant. I'm driving."

With a quick look back at all of the police cars, officers and lights she regretted promising she'd do nothing. Perhaps she'd have to do something else like put her energy into finding the clown. Then getting him to go knock on Hanni's door and scare the shit out of her.

Wait, she didn't exactly promise to not investigate the hanging body parts. Not in those words at least.

Chapter 3

"Where were you sitting on the bus?" The police detective's voice has an attitude. She thinks she's better than me. She thinks I'm a waste of her time. She wants to go on to someone more important because in her view I know nothing. She only asks questions she's pretty sure she knows the answers to and she's pretty sure I can't give her any of the answers she wants.

I won't disappoint. "In the back seat. Th-the very last one."

"Did you have anyone with you?"

"N-no."

She makes a note in a hard covered notebook. Probably some doodle that means nothing just so that she looks like she cares. Her nails look too neat for a cop and she smells nicer than one would think. She has highlights in her dark-blond hair and red on thin lips. What kind of cop wears red lipstick? I can tell she likes taking care of herself and likes looking good. She likes the way it feels when she notices someone looking at her. I bet she works out and goes to the spa and all that vanity stuff. Does she do it for herself or someone else? There's a wedding ring on her left ring finger, but what does that really mean? She must think I'm a loser to be all alone on the tour bus. Without looking up she asks, "And what did you see?"

I force my mouth not to turn up at the edges. *I saw everything you stupid cunt! I saw Joey Love's face as she started cutting his limbs off. I relished in his screams. I bathed in his searing hot blood and then I giggled like a little girl as I had her cut her own feet off. I laughed out loud as I hung their bits and pieces from the trees like a human wind-chime and when the entire bus freaked out I came in my pants.*

The detective looks up at me with steely green eyes. Can she see the real me? Can she sense it with her keen instincts?

"I-I heard that one woman scream. The one in the front." *It made me get instantly hard.* "Then I heard some others and by the time I looked people in the front were s-standing and the bus was backing up. Wha-what did they see?"

She gives me a look that says I was better off not knowing. "Bad things. You're better off not having seen them. Thank you for your time. You're the last one, so the bus is going to take you all out now." She turns away probably forgetting that she even spoke to me.

I walk to the tour bus walking past it and joining the other people who had come to watch what was going on. They collect behind the yellow police line. People from the press. People who heard about it on social media. People who don't have a life. I am merely one of them, blending in. I wear my skin like human camouflage. I'm there, but their eyes fly past me like the dirty spot on the wall that has

just "always been there." People step in front of me
without a Canadian, "Excuse me." They don't see me, the
police don't see me and the detective forgot I existed the
moment she turned around.

They're all players in my show and I, The Director, am
hidden in plain sight.

The people in the gawking crowd don't know what is
amongst them. I could take any one of them if I wanted to.
I could wait until one were to wander from the herd and
then take them without even the blond detective knowing. I
swerve around them, sizing them up and they don't see me.
What people don't actually see, but which is directly in
front of them, is amazing.

I catch sight of the tour guide. She marches behind a
man on the other side of the police line. As they duck
under the yellow tape I step back and let them go past.
They don't see me. I'm nothing to them. As I turn and
watch them I see her, the screamer. She's steps from the
driver's side of a blue Dodge 4x4. Written on the side is
The Alcrest Gastropub with a red lion ready to pounce
above the words. I've eaten there.

I liked the story of what happened there.

If the detective were to take a picture of the onlookers
like they do on the TV shows she'd see all but me looking
in her direction. I'm more interested in what comes next.

Chapter 4

Jessie parked her yellow Volkswagen Beetle beside Spencer's truck behind the restaurant. She took in a deep breath and exhaled slowly. Walking into The Alcrest had been increasingly difficult over the past year. There were good times of course, but those were becoming increasingly difficult to find.

"Jessie!" Gordie sat outside the back door to the restaurant on a turned over bucket. His large frame seemed comical on the pail. He wore black chef pants which sat low and a baggy white chef coat with his name and Sous Chef embroidered on his chest. The jacket was stained, of course. If he wasn't wearing the coat Jessie would have seen a lot more of Gordie's underwear than she has ever wanted to see. "You missed a crazy night last night."

"I heard." She glanced up the outside wood stairs that went to the apartment above. "It's all on the radio. Did you really find a dead body?"

"Parts of one. There was a head and arms and I swear there were three lower legs. Feet and all." He took a drag from a rolled cigarette. Gordie had a bushy beard of the same copper curls as his hair that was currently underneath a yellow bandana. He tossed the smoke on the ground and crushed it with the toe of his kitchen clog before pushing himself up.

"That better have been just a cigarette."

Gordie smiled. "I save the fun stuff for after work."

"I thought for you kitchen types work was the fun stuff."

"Not lately. After you."

The unique thing of this restaurant was that the kitchen was out in the dining room, so through the back door was the dishpit area. The small room had 3 sinks, a small industrial dishwasher and a stainless steel prep table with shelves above it holding dried goods and spices. There was also a door to the internal stairs leading to the apartment, the chef's open doorway and a large metal door that led to the walk-in cooler. The walls were white tile for easy clean-up.

The cooler door opened and Spencer stepped out with two plastic containers in his hands. He looked at the two of them as he crossed and dropped the containers on the pile of dirty dishes in the sink in front of the dishwasher. Brown liquid splashed up onto the wall. He didn't look like he was in a good mood. His eyes passed over Jessie and fell on his sous chef. "Who made the salmon marinade?"

Gordie shrugged his shoulders. "I did, I guess."

"It's sour. I can't use it and the pieces of salmon that were in it are ruined. It's dated three days ago. What went wrong?" Spencer's voice was raised. "This should be good for a week, at least."

"I don't know, man."

"Did you use the recipe?"

"Yeah."

Spencer bit his lip. "Did you read and follow the recipe or just go from memory?"

Jessie slipped into the office to hang up her coat and get out of the line of fire.

"I did what I always do." Gordie plucked his apron from the edge of the dishpit table – nobody ever wore them outside.

"Did you read it from the recipe?" Spit flew from Spencer's lips.

"Spencer, calm down," Jessie said.

Spencer held a finger up toward her. He never let his eyes leave Gordie. "The recipe is there for a reason. It's sour after three days, so something went wrong." He'd never bitched at his sous chef like this before. The Sous Chef was his second in command. He knew as much, if not more, than the chef and could easily stand in when needed. Spencer didn't like getting angry at anyone, however it was becoming his go-to response. "Just follow the recipes."

"We shouldn't even have recipes. Whatever happened to changing the menu all the time and making things up? We've had the same salmon dish for three weeks."

"Well I guess we won't be serving it tonight, will we? Get to work."

Jessie waited for Gordie to head down the hallway toward the dining room and kitchen before confronting the chef. "Is something wrong, Spencer? I've never heard you talk to him like that."

Spencer and Jessie had not really been a couple since around Christmas. She did come upstairs once in a while, but never stayed overnight. Last summer she had aborted their child and his anger had been growing ever since.

He couldn't get his thoughts straight. "Maybe it's about time I talked to him like that. Everyone's had it too easy around here and I'll talk to my staff however I want to. That includes you. Don't contradict me in front of them." He stared right at her.

Jessie stared back for a long moment. "Do you want to tell me what happened last night?"

"Chrys Alcrest happened. She came up with a plan and everything got fucked up."

Jessie's eyes seemed to fade into shadow. Her lips moved as if she was about to say something. She pushed them together, turned and marched down the hallway.

Spencer threw out the salmon and ran a tray of dirty dishes through the dishwasher before following.

Nobody got it. This was his place and he had to find the ways to make it work. If that meant having the same menu day after day then that was what he had to do. If it meant raising his voice and bitching people out, that was what was going to happen. He didn't like getting mad, but sometimes you had to take that path. He was their boss, not their friend or lover.

When Spencer took over The Alcrest he put the focus onto the food, got rid of the old-timers who'd sit there all night nursing the same mug of beer, brought in local artists work for the walls, singer-songwriters to perform, different clubs used it as a meeting place and he catered to a younger more sophisticated clientele. It worked for a while, but the economy and having a headless body burnt to a crisp in an oven put a damper on things. Some staff left. Quite a few clients tried elsewhere. A few of the groups that met there on a regular basis stopped being so regular. He didn't charge them anyway, so it was nothing off them. He did miss the drinks and food they would purchase, however. He had to come up with a new plan.

Passing through the hallway with the bathrooms they came out into the open dining room. The hostess stand beside a glass baking display was the first thing you came to. The same baker that had worked for Spencer's father came in every morning before the place was open to make muffins, cookies and other goodies for the morning crowd and then she would also cook a simple breakfast. Today's muffin special was orange-cranberry. Her fresh banana bread was almost gone. The only meal time that was still successful was the morning commute to work and Spencer was certain that was just because of the baking. The kitchen and small bar ran along one wall with a barrier and walkway keeping it from the tables and chairs which made an L shape around them. In the opposite corner there was a small stage for the local musicians on Friday's and Saturdays. Off the main room was the Frame room. It had couches and a bookshelf with books and board games. It got its title from the wall of mostly open window frames connected to each other and suspended from the ceiling. There was another door there leading into the private dining room for groups or meetings. It hadn't been used in a while. The air had the smell of baking, garlic and that grill smell from the charbroiler. Spencer loved it. This was home to him. This was where he spent his youth instead of skateboarding or video games. He learned how to tell the difference between rare and medium steaks and that well-done was an affront to the cooking Gods before how to ride a bike. He had made it more modern while still keeping the classic feel. Losing it was not an option.

It was almost 11:00am. They only had three customers at the moment. Two people were playing a board game in the Frame room and Mr. O was sitting by the window with the blinds at half-mast. He'd probably be there most of the day writing in his notebook. In a half hour they would open for lunch and if lucky fill half the tables.

"How's everything going?" Spencer ignored his former girlfriend and stepped through the thin opening into the kitchen. The space between the cooking equipment (stove range, deep fryers, and charbroiler) and the butcher's-block countertops was called The Line. Only the cooks entered the hot, violent, magical place. It was thin so that they would turn from the stove to the butcher's-block with minimal movement.

Ranger gave the chef a nod. Sometimes that was the best anyone could get out of the skinny man (compared to everyone else he was still a kid.) He had his Alcrest cap down low over bushy eyebrows. His chef jacket looked too big for his body and was buttoned all the way up to his neck.

Spencer's fit just right. He wore his short sleeve one with the top button open. It showed off his athletic arms and the tattoos on both forearms. "It's good? This the Pico de Gallo? These cuts have to be more precise." His voice was raising again. His fingers raked through the insert of diced tomato and onion. A few were bigger than they should have been – as far as French culinary standards went. "Do you know what they'd do to this in culinary school? They'd tell you its shit and throw it out making you do it again and again until it's a perfect brunoise. You know what that is right? Three millimeter cubes. Where's the jalapeno? The cilantro? The lime zest?"

Ranger put his knife down and twisted his hands into his black pinstriped apron. "I didn't get to them yet."

"You have to go faster. We open in thirty minutes for lunch. Tequila shrimp tacos are on the menu, so we need this done. Is the shredded lettuce done yet?" Spencer tipped his face to the side trying to look in his cook's eyes.

"Yes, Chef."

"Is the slaw done?"

"Yes, Chef."

"Then we just need this done?"

"Yes, Chef."

"Get it done then. I'll give you ten minutes."

"Yes, Chef." Ranger brought up a bowl with a handful of jalapenos, limes and cilantro from under the countertop. He sliced the jalapenos in half and started seeding them right away.

Gordie and Mallory watched quietly from their stations. As Spencer turned to face them they rapidly went back to work.

Spencer remembered seeding and cutting jalapenos and other hot peppers for the cooks when his father ran the place. None of them told him to wash his hands before going to the bathroom. They all had a good laugh at his expense when he was walking funny. He couldn't remember the last time someone pulled a practical joke on anyone. "Make sure you wash your hands before touching your eyes or anything."

At 11:45am with no customers, even the board game guys left, he went to his office. The paperwork was done for the week. All of the staff were getting paid this week. Most of the vendors would get what they were owed. The butcher was going to have to be pushed back again.

Spencer had talked to the owner about him going in the butcher shop a couple times a week and working off what he owed. The fisherman he got salmon from was going to bring his wife in for a free meal to pay for last week. It wasn't his fault some of the fish was ruined. Spencer wasn't sure what he was going to do this week. He estimated he was losing two to three thousand dollars a month. Something had to bring this around. He probably had six months left of survival.

After 12:00pm Spencer went out to the kitchen to see if they needed help. Two tables of two. That was it. He stepped into the kitchen to hear the end of Gordie's story.

"I swear the woman was so dry from sitting out in the sun that she looked like an over baked salmon." He leaned back with his backside propped against the counter. Ranger stood with his hands in his pockets and Mallory was behind the cold-side table straightening things that didn't need straightening. "I swear if you cut her open dust would have come out."

Aquamarine eyes surveyed the room. Jessie was by the front plus one server on duty. Three cooks and only four customers. He was spending more than he was making.

"What are you guys doing?" Spencer's voice was enough to make Ranger pop his hands out of the pockets and take a step back.

"There's no customers," Gordie said. The smile behind his beard was gone.

"Is all the prep for tonight done? You could be cleaning, organizing. Look at Mallory."

She had everything on her table organized by height and size.

"She has OCD! That don't count. We have time to do what we need to do for tonight." The only thing Gordie changed about his stance was to cross his thick arms over his chest.

Spencer bit his lip. Mom always said to count to ten when you got angry. He made it to eight. "Not any more. All of you take the afternoon off and be back for 4:00pm." He turned and stepped out of the kitchen.

"Wait, Spencer," Gordie moved past the junior cook and leaned on the low walls on either side of the kitchen entrance. It was made that way so people going to the washroom could see all the action as they passed. "Another day of three and a half hours missed from our pay checks? That's twice this week. I don't know about these guys, but I can't keep doing this. I owe people."

"Your dealers?" Sometimes if Spencer said that it would be a joke. This time the Sous Chef stared at the Chef and didn't say a word. "I'm spending more than I'm making, Gordie. I don't like it either."

Jessie waited until the other cooks were gone before going to the chef office. "Are you okay, Spencer," she asked for the second time today.

Spencer looked up from the papers on his desk. "Call me if a customer comes in."

Chapter 5

"I have news!" Chrys suddenly appeared in front of her brother across the pass.

Spencer looked up from the plates he was about to slide between them. The food orders passed one way and the finished plates passed the other, hopefully never staying long under the hanging heat-lamps. "Do you know what time it is?" He was getting the strangest feeling of Deja vous. How often has Chrys shown up late for work with some great idea or amazing news?

Chrys put her billfold and hands on the warm tile tinking the ring on her thumb against it. She was dressed in tight black trousers and the black dress shirt of the server's uniform. The top two buttons were open. Her hair was tied back. "I have news about Leigh Park." Her full lips formed into a bright smile. "I got an ID on the victim."

Spencer ignored what his sister was saying. "It's almost seven. We have reservations. You were supposed to start work at five. Izzy, foods up." Spencer took a quick drink from the yogurt container under the pass. Glassware was a no-no on the line.

Chrys' hands dropped to her sides. She stepped back to let the server (who probably arrived on time for work) get her plates.

As Spencer passed the plates across he eyed the billfold his sister left on his pass. It held her book of order chits, all orders were hand written, and probably a few pens. He hated servers leaving stuff on the pass. Right now he despised his sister leaving anything anywhere.

Izzy said, "Fire table twelve," before walking away.

"Thank you," Spencer responded. "Fire striploin medium, penne with butternut squash, Alcrest salad." The other cooks called out their parts of the order indicating that they had heard. "On the pass in eight minutes."

"Don't you want to know who the poor bastard was?" The warmth of Chrys' expression had melted away as she retook her place. "There were two victims by the way. They identified the head and limbs, but one leg didn't belong to him. Not unless he had three feet or one majorly deformed penis. It was a woman's leg." Spencer had turned his back to her and gone back to cooking. She wasn't even sure if he could hear her over the buzz in the quarter filled room, the noises the cooks made and the sound of the exhaust fan above the equipment. "Come on. I got this info even before the press."

"Who?"

Chrys smiled. He was getting the mystery itch. "His name was Joey Love. He had been arrested for drug possession, so they got an identification quick from the fingerprints."

"I meant, who gave you the info?" Spencer dropped the penne noodles in the pot of boiling water on the back burner. It had perforated wedge shaped inserts, so once the

46

pasta was done all he had to do was lift a wedge and let it drain. He had butternut squash pasta sauce warming in a sauté pan.

"A friend. I have friends who tell me things."

Spencer stared at his sister. His fingers gripped the butcher-block counter top so hard they hurt. "I thought you weren't going to be looking into this. You said you wouldn't. You told the detective -"

"I can't stop people from telling me things." Miss Innocent.

"Order in." Hanni put a chit on the pass. "Are you working tonight, Chrys? I'm supposed to be bartending, not serving your tables." She wore the same shirt as the other servers with the obvious addition of a push-up bra and a mini-skirt, which barely hid anything, instead of the trousers.

"Whatever. You get bigger tips this way anyway and you can strut around showing off your ass."

"I'd rather be behind the bar getting a view of your brother's ass." Hanni put her nose close to Chrys'. "Need another drink, Spence?"

Chrys turned to her brother. "Are you drinking alcohol? You're working! Are you giving him alcohol?"

Spencer ignored both of them.

"He's a grown man, Chrys. He can do what he wants."

"Just keep your eyes and claws off of him." The two women stared at each other a long moment before the blond walked away. Chrys kept staring at her. She couldn't remember the reasoning behind saving her from a drug overdose last summer. Temporary insanity. As she looked at her brother she wondered if he had heard everything.

47

"Izzy, table twelve." Spencer slid the penne with butternut squash under the heat lamp. Mallory had the salad on her table and Gordie slid the steak with potatoes and vegetables under the heat lamp in front of him. Everything in the kitchen was about timing. At least they had that part right.

"What's wrong?" Spencer completely ignored his sister the moment he saw the tears welling in Izzy's eyes.

As she picked the plates up her hands trembled. "That table of two in the corner? The guy with the beard. He grabbed me."

"Chrys, deliver these plates to table twelve."

"What?" Chrys' mouth dropped.

Spencer glared at his sister. His own eyes were glassy but that was anger, not tears. "I wasn't asking you Chrys. Izzy, come with me." He stepped through the entry between the hot line and the bar. His hands went into fists at his sides as he walked straight toward the small table in the corner. The two men were talking to each other about some sport. The other one looked at the chef but the one with the beard continued talking. "Excuse me."

"Yeah?"

Both had steaks on their plates with half of the meal gone.

"I think you need to apologize to my server."

Without a pause the one in the beard said, "fuck you," and took a drink of his beer.

Spencer breathed out of his nose. His dimples were gone. He stared at the man and wondered in his head what Gordon Ramsay would do. "Izzy, take a break."

As the man put the beer down Spencer reached out and plucked his plate from the table. He slammed it down onto the other man's plate. Meat juices and mashed potato squirted out onto the table. Both men flinched back. "Finish your drinks and leave." He turned with the plates in hand, marched past the kitchen and into the back where he put the plates down in the dishpit and washed his hands.

As he returned to the kitchen he saw the two men were gone. Probably didn't pay for what they had either.

"Those two guys wanted me to tell you to go fuck yourself," Gordie said as his boss squeezed past him.

"Whatever." Spencer got back into his position organizing the orders. "Where are we?"

Gordie pointed to the closest chit with his tongs. "This table, Chef." It was said with a little respect in his voice.

"What the hell was that?" Chrys' voice squealed.

Spencer turned back to his sister. He had heard every word between her and Hanni. He also heard everything she said about the dead people. She had promised things and was going back on it. They weren't kids any more, but even in adulthood promises had to mean something. Plus she was now getting into his personal business. His eyes dropped to the warm tiles.

He reached back and grabbed his tongs from the oven door. They were an extension of a chef's arm like metal lobster claws. The tongs grabbed the billfold. With a flick of his wrist the leather bound folder flew into the air. Pens shot out. The chit bills fell free. The entire mess hit his sister's arm before dropping to the floor. Pieces of paper rode air waves under the closest tables.

Chrys stared at him. Everyone was probably watching her. She had to control her breaths. She had to control her emotions. Her teeth clamped down on her lip hoping the pain would stop her from crying. She dropped to her knees

49

and started gathering everything. She had to crawl to get chits under the closest table forcing the people sitting there to move their feet. She could feel Hanni laughing at her from across the room.

"Get to work," was all she heard from the other side of the pass.

Chrys got to her feet. Her entire body shook. She tried counting. As she saw Spencer's blue-green eyes she forgot what came after four. Her hand flicked out. The billfold Frisbeed over the pass and toward her brother's face. He was fast enough to block it, but that just sent the papers doing their dance onto the butcher-block counter and kitchen line floor. One chit landed on the stovetop and burst into flame.

Yeah, everything was going to hell.

Chapter 6

"My brother's an ass! That looks nice."

"No, g'day? Nothing like that?"

Chrys looked at her girlfriend with innocent puppy eyes. "I said that looks nice." She paced around the room. Chrys didn't even bother going upstairs to the apartment. She stormed out the back door of the restaurant, circled around the front of the building and ran across the street to Expressions Tattoo. She hoped Spencer saw her, but the blinds were down in the dining room.

Sloane put her concentration back into the tattoo she was putting on a man's bicep. The Australian had started to work at the tattoo parlor last summer and both women fell for each other. Chrys had been in relationships with both sexes through her twenty-six years. She still wasn't certain which way she would end up going and sticking with. Since the last man she dated was a murder suspect he was happy with the way things were at the moment.

"I know you're dying to tell me, so go ahead. Why is your bro an ass?" Sloane's accent was thick and lovely.

"He just is. He thinks the restaurant's all his, so he does what he wants."

The buzz of the tattoo machine mixed with the dance beats coming from a phone hooked up to speakers. The room had white walls with copies of Sloane's work tacked all over. Chrys' chrysanthemum tattoo was in the top right. Behind the artist was a black and turquois toolbox just like the giant ones you would see in a mechanics garage. Two shelves held every colour of ink you could imagine. Sloane looked up. "He is the owner, isn't he?"

"Whatever." Chrys' arms flew out at her sides. "That's not the point. It's called The Alcrest Gastropub. Alcrest. I'm an Alcrest. Maybe not in blood but in name I am. I should get a say in what goes on there as much as he does."

"But he's the owner," Sloane tried to keep her smile hidden as she worked on her art.

"And I think he's been drinking on the job."

"That's not good, but he's the boss."

If asked, the guy in the chair (who looked like he would never be caught in a tattoo shop) would have had a difficult time deciding which one was better looking. Chrys had the girl-next-door look going for her while the tattoo artist had an androgynist beauty augmented and enhanced by several tattoos on her body.

"Whose side are you on, Sloane?"

"I'm not on anyone's side. He's your brother and at that restaurant he's your boss."

"Probably not after tonight." Chrys went over what happened across the street. "And I just left. He probably doesn't even know I'm not coming back. I don't care. I don't need the money or anything." Chrys couldn't stand still. She felt her phone vibrate in her back pocket. It was probably going to be somebody at the restaurant. Where are you? Are you coming back?

"Did you tell him about your other job?"

"No! God no. He'd kill me if he knew where I was working. He's always downstairs before I leave, so I don't even think he knows I go to work every day. There's no reason he should be upset about my job. It's not like its illegal or anything."

"Tell him then."

Chrys didn't speak another word about it. Spencer would insist she quit and she had enough of him running her life. She was independent and hated anyone telling her what to do. She had to do something other than waitressing for the rest of her life. The dancing – she had gone about as far as she could in this city teaching a few nights a week at the Elizabeth Frances Dance Studio. Roller-derby – she wasn't much into it anymore and you didn't make money at it. Modeling and acting – she wasn't really into those either. The thing that gave her the biggest rush lately was investigating murders and strange occurrences. Her new boss gave her the information on the dead bodies, but she did tell her brother she wouldn't look into it and she didn't feel right going back on that. Even if he was a dick.

Chrys bent down to look at the design developing on the arm. It was a dragon's body almost tying itself into a knot. "Do you want to go clown searching tonight?"

"Alright. I've got another hour here if you want to come back."

"Shiny!" Chrys knew her brother was probably busy. Especially since he had become one of those chef's that insisted on doing everything himself. The street out front had a few cars and the parking lot in the back was a third full. She wouldn't have to run into him if she took the back stairs to the apartment. She quickly changed her clothes and gathered the dogs to take them for a walk.

She carried Breeze, her Chihuahua, down the stairs while Spencer's bulldog, Bullet, took each step one at a time pausing on each before attempting the next one. As soon as they all hit the ground Breeze took off to the end of her leash. Bullet was already panting and trudged along beside Chrys' feet.

She took them into the side street behind the restaurant. It was all residential. It was probably not the best place to have the restaurant, you didn't get the drive-by traffic, but The Alcrest and most of the small businesses on their street had been there a long time. Sooner or later it would be over for them. She hoped for later.

As the street lights came on she headed for home. The only time she stopped was to give someone directions. It was a much different neighborhood than what she worked in at her secret job. That place was not safe at night. Her home neighborhood was fine.

Chapter 7

"C-can you give me a hand? I'm trying to find 435 Sc-scoble Avenue." I don't smile. People worried about finding where they need to go don't smile. "I turned somewhere and I'm lost."

If you drove a mini-van you were less intimidating. If you only rolled the window down half-way you were being a little wary of the person outside. You had to be unassuming. You had to make them think you were being cautious of them. A baby on board sticker never hurt. The flowers painted on the side said I was just a delivery guy.

"Sure." The woman turned away from me to point. My ruse worked. "Go down here to Pearson and turn right."

I don't listen. I look. I'm aware of how she moves. She has muscle and good reactions. She'd put up a fight. I see the scar on her upper arm and her misshapen right earlobe. I see the curves of her body. I could easily stun her now and get her in the back of the van before anyone would notice. The one dog would yap. The other is fat enough to make a good roast. If I left the dogs, someone would notice. Someone would call the police. A search would start. That wasn't how I played the game. She isn't who I want anyway. She's just a bit player in this play. An extra. She wouldn't scream. And I'm not a fan of dark meat.

"I think to get to 435, you hang a left on Scoble. Pretty sure."

She doesn't recognize me. Yesterday she looked at my ticket, gave me her best welcoming smile and told me to climb on board and have a seat. She looks right at me and doesn't see through my human camouflage. It's always the pretty ones who can't see. In school they never notice you. That's what makes them easy to take.

"Thank you. N-nice looking dogs. Have a nice night." Now is the time to give her a smile and an awkward wave.

I drive away and in the rear-view mirror can tell she doesn't look at the license plate of this simple business vehicle. She doesn't even think twice about it. Why should she? She might remember seeing the van, but she doesn't remember me and that's what counts. She doesn't see. It's just a nice night in a nice neighborhood.

Chapter 8

"Are you okay, Spence?"

As he looked up from the receipts on his desk he found Jessie leaning against the door frame. Her eyes looked dark. When she was in a melancholy mood shadows seemed to fall over them giving her that naturally smoky look women paid money to achieve. She had her arms crossed in front of her, sleeves rolled up to the elbows. He could barely see the tattoo along her forearm, "candle within the chaos." That's what he thought she was to him. Then she ended something that could have been special. He wasn't sure if he even wanted it, but she ended it without a word to him. That blew the candle out.

"I'm fine, why?"

"Just asking." Her short sun-kissed hair fell down over her brow as she dropped her gaze. "You sure there's nothing you want to talk about?"

"Nope."

"You've never thrown customers out before."

"They deserved it."

Spencer knew her next move. She would flick her hair back, smile and the shadow of her eyes would fade away. Then she'd tell him she would see him tomorrow in her sexy husky voice and he would sit there for a while thinking he should call her back. It had gone that way for months.

"Spence," she didn't lift her head.

His stomach tightened. His head was spinning. He had a bit of a buzz on from what was in his yogurt container during service. He had no excuse for drinking while working except that he needed it to cope with everything. He liked to think it numbed things. As he focused on Jessie's face and watched her eyes change he knew he wasn't going to be happy.

"I'm seeing someone. We've only been on a couple of dates, but I think it's going to go somewhere."

Spencer wasn't sure why he suddenly felt like tossing all of the night's receipts off his desk and screaming. He didn't do it. He sat still. He stared across at her not sure what he was feeling. Was this anger or jealousy? Perhaps a little relief.

Jessie flicked her head back. Her hair flipped up and to the side. It half slipped back over her forehead. Her eyes didn't seem to have that shadow effect any more. "I wanted to tell you myself before you found out. You know how everyone here talks. Anyway, the front is all locked up. I'll see you tomorrow."

Spencer mumbled, "night." The word barely passing his lips.

He sat there for a long time staring at the empty doorway. He wasn't upset that Jessie was dating. He was upset because he always thought she would be there for him. A fall back. That wasn't a way to think of someone, but that was what he thought. And now she wasn't going to be. What did that leave him with?

Who was he becoming?

Everything was a mess. It was more than Jessie. Even on the hot line he wasn't sure any more. He fell in love with cooking as a little kid working with the rough pub cooks Dad hired that put good food together in a sloppy way, played jokes on each other and were crude and rude even with a ten year old around. He went to culinary school with the intention of being a Jamie Oliver or Gordon Ramsay. He graduated school and worked in high end places. He had dreams. Then his Mom told him Dad was ill. Spencer went home and started doing his duty as a son. His father passed and he bought The Alcrest from his mother. He had dreams then that included the gastropub. He was having trouble remembering them now.

Jessie had been part of those dreams. He had wanted her to be. He didn't always tell or show her though. Something was always in the way. He was.

Chrys was part of the dream too. She was his sister. He loved her, however at the moment he didn't want to be anywhere near her.

Things felt like they were imploding. The dreams were crumbling. He couldn't control anything. He couldn't even control himself.

After being tortured and having his friend killed he started drinking to forget. At first it was after work to take the edge off. Then occasionally in the morning to cope with the reality of the day. His father would have fired anyone on the spot for drinking while on the line. He tried not to, but he felt like he needed it. He had to forget everything bad and it helped him focus.

Somehow Spencer found himself in his truck driving the Middleton streets after sending a text asking a friend if he could come over. He didn't want to be home laying in the bed he had shared with Jessie. All he would do there would be to think about what bills needed to be paid, what he couldn't pay, how long they could last the way they were going. While trying not to ask himself if Jessie was with her new guy?

He maneuvered his truck around a mini-van and stopped next to the curb. What was he doing?

He stepped out into the cool air that cleaned out his brain for a moment. Something was wrong. This whole thing was wrong. He had that eerie feeling that he needed to turn around. He was too afraid of what would be there.

It was a nice neighborhood of homes and up-kept lawns. Average looking automobiles sat in driveways and on the street in front of average looking houses. A few yards had dimming solar powered lights. Garden gnomes stood vigil around a couple flower beds and gardens. The front yard of the house he was at had recently been mowed. That was all the upkeep there was. A sign in the yard and in a second floor window announced apartment for rent. The air was chilly. Sweater weather, as his mom would say. You could almost feel the rain coming.

He knocked on the front door. Hanni had the ground floor of the house. Someone else lived upstairs or did.

Spencer felt a bead of sweat run down from his temple. He took a deep breath and let it out. The door opened. He held his breath.

"Hi," Hanni said. She sipped red wine from a glass before holding it out for her guest.

Spencer took it and swallowed a healthy amount. Hanni had cleaned off her make-up and had changed into shorts and a thin tank-top cut-out enough on the sides to expose the roundness of her breasts underneath. The moment the cool air hit her, her nipples pressed against the fabric. Even without all of the outer coatings she looked great. Long – thin legs, breasts that were a lot smaller without the push-ups (they were more approachable this way) and her hair falling free around her face and over her shoulders. She wasn't the seductive waitress trying to shock and get a bigger tip. She was just a woman. He handed the wine back to her. The French-tipped nails tinked against the glass.

Hanni wasn't sure why he was there. He just said he want to talk. "Do you want to come in?" Her nose scrunched as she sniffed.

No, he didn't.

His left hand cupped her face as the other grasped her waist and pulled her to him. Their bodies and mouths met at the same moment. He kissed her tasting the wine on her thin lips. She tasted the Crown Royal and Pepsi on his. Moist tongues began to battle. His thumb gently caressed her cheek.

She could feel the hardened callus where his knife dug into his index finger joint against her skin and the twitching of his growing erection against her stomach. She slipped her hand inside his coat, gripping his shirt and pulling him closer.

Spencer walked his hand up her body slipping it in the side cut-out of her tank. He didn't want to think about the restaurant or Jessie. He sure as hell didn't want to think about his sister. Alcohol didn't numb anything, so maybe

61

this would. He just wanted to feel something other than fearing bill collectors. His palm cupped Hanni's bare breast. His thumb caressed her nipple hardening it instantly.

She put the wine glass in his other hand. Her fingers grabbed the elastic of his pants and found the strings hanging loose. Chef pants were easy to get in and out of. Her nails scratched his lower belly. His abs tightened. The back of her fingers ran over his flat stomach. "You don't have to be so gentle with me," she said and slipped a hand inside the black pants grabbing what pulsed inside. She was surprised he went commando.

His breath caught.

"We should go inside." He squeezed her firm breast tight enough she let out a gasp. Her hand stroked. He felt his pants slipping. "Someone's watching." Was that panic in his voice?

Hanni peaked around him. There were cars parked on both sides of the street. Nobody was around. "Who's watching?"

"Someone." He kissed her again and tugged on her lower lip with his teeth. "Someone's watching. That's all I know." He was smiling. That was new. He nudged her back.

"Let them watch." Hanni pushed his pants down letting them slip to his knees. The air chilled his ass cheeks.

"What are you doing? Hanni!"

She took hold of his shaft and guided him in. "You have to let go, Spencer."

He threw his arm out. The fingertips barely hit the door making it swing shut.

~ * ~

A year ago Spencer was more relaxed. There were still the problems of staffing and bills and not having enough customers to be overly comfortable, however the financials were in the black. They made enough at the gastropub for him to have a little extra every month. Then there was the headless body cooked in the oven. The ovens were replaced by an old friend of his fathers who was also the alleged leader of the Irish Mafia in Middleton, but the stink was still there. The friend brought its own news stories. One thing lead to another which lead to another which lead to Spencer no longer being relaxed. First he started making sure he was downstairs when the baker arrived. It was more because she was afraid to start the ovens and look inside. Then after the summer he started staying late to count the day's receipts. Usually that was Jessie's job. He casually took it over until it was an every night thing. He had nightmares and didn't want much sleep. Up before dawn. Bed sometimes around midnight or later. Working out was something he didn't bother with any more. He was still in good shape because he was eating very little. A few times a week he got away from the restaurant to do something else. A couple hours each week when he could try and relax, but it was all still there in his mind.

It was in the early morning when everything hit him. He would wake and stare at the ceiling as everything came to him and he realized how screwed he was.

Today was fish market day. He had to be down at the docks by 5:00 am to get good buys and hopefully beat the other city chefs. They were doing new things with new cooking techniques and different tastes. Spencer was just rotating through recipes. He hated it.

"Where are you going?"

He didn't even have his feet on the floor. "Fish market." He felt fingers and their nails trace the white scars on his back. "Go back to sleep."

"Give me a kiss first."

Spencer turned back and lowered himself until his lips met Hanni's. He felt dirty. Last night had been a collection of what Jessie told him, booze and self-loathing. A lot of it was being turned on by the blond waitress, but it wasn't everything. Their tongues wrestled. Her nails scratched his back. Finally she released him and he got up. It was more like he pushed away until she let go.

His sister was going to be pissed when she found out about what he did last night and he wasn't sure how Jessie would take it. Spencer did feel…icky…about last night, but kissing Hanni, having her hands on him, knowing she was there naked beside him made everything stir and he wasn't sure he wanted to leave. He didn't want this to be an everyday thing. Maybe more of an "as you need it" thing. Yeah, that made him feel so much better.

After he was dressed in last night's chef pants and Deadpool T-shirt he took a look back at the bed. Hanni was there naked above the blankets face down and asleep. Her blond hair was tossed around her head. Her arms lay at her sides and her long legs were apart. The heart shaped buttock was extremely inviting. At night he wanted to feel her lips on him and be inside her. During the daylight hours the idea of screwing her – just the idea – made him feel filthy. It was still dark out, however.

He quickly left the apartment.

On a good day the fish market had a festival attitude. The coffee truck would be in the corner of the parking lot before you walked down onto the docks. There was usually people calling out what they had for sale, music, people cooking different fish items, chefs and restaurateurs fighting with other market owners for the best items and just regular folk looking to get a fish and see what it was all about. That was on a good day. This morning the rain had been pouring for hours. Only the diehards would be out today. The coffee truck was still open though.

Spencer wrapped his hands around a Styrofoam cup as he headed down to the docks. It didn't smell fishy as one would think. It smelled of the salty sea. Fishermen put their catch in big bins of ice or lined them up nicely in Styrofoam boxes. He took his time walking around and talking to the fishermen and dealers. He couldn't really afford much, so he might as well relax for a while.

"Early bird gets the worm, Spencer?"

He knew that voice. There goes the relaxation. "That's the idea, Garrett." Spencer had graduated from the Culinary Institute of Canada with the chef of Legend Restaurant. "How are you doing?"

"Pretty damn good. Restaurant is full every night. My wife is pregnant. And I'm in some dealings about a second restaurant downtown. It's all pretty exciting. You?" It was like he knew everything that was crashing in Spencer's life.

"I'm doing well." Spencer sipped at his coffee. He felt Garrett's eyes on him.

"You look ruffled around the edges, Spence. That either means a good night or a bad one." His laugh was so fake.

When Spencer smiled his dimples showed. He looked around hoping to find someone else to talk to. It wasn't that

65

he didn't want to talk to Garrett, but every second day he heard or read something good about Legend and the "chef on the rise." They may have graduated from the same place, but most definitely took different paths. "I hear you pilfered some of my staff."

"Oh come on. They came to me, Spence. I'd never go out looking to steal your crew. Look, why don't you come by the restaurant. Bring your sister. My treat."

"Maybe I will." Spencer didn't want to offer the same thing. His friend had expensive tastes and wouldn't feel a twinge of guilt fulfilling them on Spencer's dime.

Two servers had left The Alcrest for the fancy restaurant with its high prices and small portions. People kept telling Spencer to raise his prices, but that wasn't the idea of The Alcrest. Great high end food at affordable prices in a friendly atmosphere. At least that was the original idea. He remembered arguing with his father after coming back from culinary school that the food needed to be elevated to more than deep fried and grilled.

Spencer bought an 80lb halibut from Hans, his main supplier, along with a box of haddock. The big halibut he could fillet and portion himself to the size he would like and use the carcass to make a nice broth. The small haddock would be great for beer battered fish and chips. At least it wasn't salmon. Maybe Gordie would be happy. He paid half the price and convinced Hans to come for dinner to pay for the rest.

He could probably go to the butchers down the street from the restaurant for some cheap cuts of meat, grind them up and make his own sausages for bangers and mash. An English themed menu could be fun. A tribute to his Dad's pub days. This was why he liked coming down here. It gave his mind a chance to relax and his creativity to bloom.

As he helped Hans' son lift the plastic tub with the halibut into the back of his truck Spencer was thinking of how he could pan sear it in butter. Maybe put it with asparagus or a medley of spring vegetables and new potatoes.

He opened the front door. He could do a shepherd's pie for the menu. Simple. Classic.

"What the fuck!" Spencer leapt from the truck.

His shoes shuffled on the wet pavement. His heart raced. One hand still held onto the open door. Rain splashed against it and the seat inside. With wide eyes he looked around. There was nobody near him. Nobody was watching. Hans' son was walking away and was almost to the coffee truck.

Spencer looked inside the cab of his truck. It was a twin cab. The seat in the back was folded down so that he could store groceries on it. There was a string stretched from one back door to the other. He had never seen that before. He also never saw what was hanging from it.

The two arms were tied at the fingers in a grotesque peace sign. The nails had yellow polish on them. Between them was a foot. The string was tied to a toe. On the far side was a ball of blond hair. The strands hung down over what he assumed was a head. The hair was more dirty than blond. As he stared it turned slightly and he saw a milky eye staring back at him. The wind blew into the cab making the body parts swing and bounce against each other. Blood dripped from the hacked joints. Even with the rain falling he heard it land. Drip.

Chapter 9

"You're kidding me, right?" Detective Washburn sat in the front seat of her car. The rain had stopped, so her door was open and her feet out. She slipped off a high heel and replaced it with a running shoe.

Spencer looked at her from the back seat. Rain water still dripped onto his face from his short blond hair. "About what?" He was soaked right through. After calling the police he stood out behind the truck letting the rain fall on him. He was stunned. He didn't know what to do and all he could see was that milky eye.

"You're at the other scene and now this. It's all a joke, right? You and your sister are playing a joke on me?"

"I don't find it funny."

"Me neither. So you did your shopping or fishing or whatever the fuck you call it and came back to a truck full of body parts. That about it?" Her green eyes stared at him through the rearview mirror as she pulled on the last shoe. She turned in the seat and looked at him directly. "You're sure they weren't there before you got down here?"

"Yeah, I'm pretty sure I would have noticed. I got in my truck at," he looked out the side window to avoid her eyes, "a friends and had to back up. I'm pretty sure I would have noticed, damn it."

"Calm down, Dimples. I'm the good guy, remember?"

Spencer watched her get out of the car and smooth out the wrinkles in her slacks. Her changing her shoes was the sexiest imitation of Mr. Rogers he had ever seen. He couldn't tell her age. She looked around the same as him, thirty-two, but facial lines stamped in her face said a different story.

"Were there any signs of someone breaking in? Broken lock, open window?"

"No. I didn't see anything."

She looked down at him still sitting in the back of her car. "Do you think they had a key? Does your sister have a key?"

He slowly lifted his head. "She's crazy, but she's not that crazy. There's usually a lot of people down here, so I might have not locked it. I don't know. Any idea who that was," he pointed toward his truck, "Detective Washburn?"

"Call me Wash. I'm thinking these limbs belong to the extra foot from the other night. The toe nails have the same chipped polish." She had already taken a quick look before having him sit in her car. "Hopefully we can identify her."

"Who do you think is doing this?"

"That's the question."

"Is he going to kill again?"

"And that's another question. My big questions are where are the torso's and why does this all seem to be focused on you." Wash wasn't wearing her glasses today making her eyes razor sharp when they focused on Spencer.

"You were on the bus. Now body parts in your truck. It all seems a little more than coincidental. Does the name Joey Love sound familiar?"

"No." Damn Chrys.

"Are you sure?" She took out her phone and brought up a picture of a thin man with hard cheek bones and stubble on his jaw. He had dark eyes and stringy brown hair. His cheeks looked hallow. He wasn't pretty.

Spencer was just glad the picture was while he was still alive. "No. He doesn't look familiar."

"Not even from that group that tortured you last year? I read they weren't all found and they were all ex-cons."

He pushed himself from the car. He could barely see his truck with all the police vehicles and crime scene people around it. He wasn't sure what was going to happen with it. Was a hanging corpse covered under insurance? He said, "I was a bit pre-occupied with things, but he doesn't look like the type of employee they would have hired. They weren't into employing drugies."

Wash took a solid stance. Her arms crossed over her chest. "Who said he was on drugs? Are you holding out on me, Dimples?"

He thought, damn you Chrys, again. "No, he just looks like he probably did. Do you really think this killer is focused on me? Are we in danger?"

"Well, you still have all your body parts, so you can't be in that much danger. I just can't see how this can be a coincidence. I'll be right back."

This had to have something to do with those people that tortured him. But then how did they know he would be on the ghost tour? How could they have set that up? He didn't even know he was going on that bus until that same night.

Unless his sister was in on it or she had told someone. It didn't make sense. His sister couldn't possibly be part of the killing. How was this connected to him then? Or was it Chrys?

Spencer stared across the parking lot. The other chefs were gone. He didn't see when Garrett left. The fish that didn't sell this morning was put into trucks and shipped to grocery stores and markets around the city. The coffee truck was still there selling drinks to police officers and people who came to see what was happening. People were taking pictures with their phones and posting them on social media or sending them to friends. Spencer wasn't sure how he felt about pictures of The Alcrest Gastropub written across the truck where body parts were found being posted all over the Internet. It was a strange world and he was tired of it.

A black limousine turned into the parking lot from the higher street. Its horn honked to make the crowd part.

Spencer looked at his truck where Detective Washburn had climbed all the way inside looking for clues. Even once the body pieces were out the question was if he'd be able to get the inside of the truck cleaned. Would there be a smell? Was he ever going to get rid of the sensation that something was there hanging behind his shoulder? Someone had been in his truck hanging body parts. Someone had hid in the back before and attacked Chrys. Maybe the truck was bad luck.

He turned back toward the crowd. The driver was out of the limo. As he opened the back door someone climbed out. Chestnut hair flicked around.

"Fuck."

72

"Spencer!" Chrys ran toward him. She was stopped at the police line. "What? That's my brother." The police officer on the side of the yellow tape she wanted to be on, started to say something. "I don't care about procedure. That's my brother over there, so let me through."

By the time Spencer got to her she had her hands next to her face and was doing sort of sign language thing as she repeated, "That's my brother," as if the problem was that the cop was deaf. She was going to get herself arrested.

"What are you doing here, Chrys?"

"This guy won't let me past this yellow tape as if it's some fucking force field." She waved her hand in front of the officer's face. "These are not the droids you are looking for."

"What are you doing here Chrys," Spencer repeated. He stayed a little behind the officer as if to say, "na, na I'm on this side and you're not." If his clothes weren't so heavy from rain and his mind full of visions of body parts he would have smiled.

Chrys sidestepped to be able to look at him. She had to push an onlooker out of her way. "I heard you were down here and what happened. You didn't come to the apartment last night, so I've been worried sick. I had to make sure you were okay."

Spencer looked his sister up and down. She wore a long skirt and a top that was clingy, covered with a blazer. On her feet were open toed heels instead of her ankle boots. Her lips were pink and her eyes defined by mascara and liner. She normally only did something to plump the lashes. This wasn't the usual Chrys at 9:00 am. That Chrys was still in bed drooling on her pillow. "Where are you coming from? Whose car is that?"

As her head spun around her loose hair flipped over her shoulders. "What? I just got to work and found out." Her voice trailed off.

"What sort of job gives you a limo?"

"I'm a receptionist. I told the boss I needed to get here quick."

"Who's your boss?"

Chrys sidestepped to look around the other side of the officer. "What's' going on here anyway?"

"Who's your boss, Chrys?" Spencer's voice was stern. His fingers flexed in and out of fists. In his mind he went through the list of people they knew that would show up in a black town-car or limousine. It was a short list.

Chrys cursed at herself. She just wanted to get down to the fishing docks to make sure her brother was okay and didn't think about the statement the car would make. After an unsuccessful clown hunt with Sloane last night, Chrys knocked on her brother's bedroom door hoping to apologize or that he would apologize to her. She found his bed empty and still made from the morning. Her brother was annoying with his cleanliness. After a couple of texts to him with no replies she went to sleep. In the morning his bed was still empty.

"Don't worry about it, Spencer. It has nothing to do with you." She was getting tired of him holding money over her head anyway. This was going to be one other thing.

"This isn't much of a surprise." Detective Washburn strolled over to them. "Let her in Wayne." She walked in front of them leading the way to her car. She turned quickly and focused her attention on Chrys. "Nice ride. Yes, there are perks for working for Liam O'Donnell."

Spencer's mouth dropped. His eyes went wide then focused to a pinpoint. His sister stared at the detective without flinching.

"I looked into you."

"What the hell? Am I a suspect?" Chrys wasn't moving. The two women stared at each other like a pair of wild-west gunfighters. Which one would flinch first?

Wash's lips formed to a wicked smile. "Everyone's a suspect until they're not. I was telling your brother that it's a strange coincidence that he was at both scenes. You were the tour guide. You could have always set it up. You know your brother comes here every Tuesday morning, so it wouldn't be hard for you to come down here and set this up too."

"Go fuck yourself!"

"Chrys!"

"Maybe working for the Irish mob is rubbing off on you." Wash continued to smile. She didn't believe any of it, but it was fun watching the young woman get all worked up.

"Kiss my tight ass, you cunt!" Chrys spun around and marched away. Her heels clicked on the pavement.

As Spencer took a step to go after his sister Wash grabbed his arm. "I was just screwing with her. Hopefully she'll keep her nose out of things now."

"Sorry about what she said."

"Why? I am a cunt."

"Still, come by The Alcrest some night and I'll buy dinner." He gave the detective a polite nod and turned his attention on his sister. She was just about at the limousine. She just cost him a dinner. Two if Wash brought her husband. He ducked the police tape and quickened his pace. He told Chrys to stay away from Liam O'Donnell more than once. His father's old friend was nothing but trouble. Spencer grabbed the back door to the limo and whipped it open. "What are you doing?"

Chrys flinched away. The leather seat creaked. Her lips snarled. "Going back to work. What's your problem?"

"This car. Your job. Your boss." Spencer had one hand on the door and the other on the car.

He suddenly felt a tug on his back. His feet left the ground as he stumbled. His body was spun around. A weight was pressed on Spencer's chest as he was pushed back until his backside hit the car. The driver of the limo was right there in his face, so close Spencer could smell his minty breath and feel the gun shaped lump under his jacket. He pushed back.

The driver shoved his whole weight against the chef making him bend back over the car.

Chrys shimmied out of the car and grabbed at the driver's coat. He wasn't moving. "Glenn, stop it."

The driver's hands let go of Spencer immediately. He took a step back. His eyes never left the chef's though.

"He's my brother. He gets mad, a lot. He's a dick, but he'd never hurt me." She gave up on tugging Glenn's arm and stroked it instead until he returned to the driver's side of the vehicle. Chrys reached out to touch her brother's arm. "We can talk about this tonight."

He pulled away. He stood still, except for the shakes he couldn't control, and stared out at the boats in the harbor. "I told you what I think. I have to go. I have a restaurant to run."

"I can get Glenn to give you a ride. I'm sure Mr. O'Donnell won't mind."

Spencer laughed. "No, I'm good."

"Whatever." Chrys sat back down in the back seat of the limousine. She carefully held her knees together as she lifted them inside the car. She paused for one second than had her legs out not caring about her knees or who saw what. "Where the hell were you last night? You didn't sleep at home. Did you and Jessie patch things up?"

He stared at her. He tried his best not to show any expression. "No, we didn't."

"Then where were you, Spence?"

"Nowhere. Like you said, don't worry about it. I'm fine."

"Where did you sleep?"

Spencer watched his sister's face. He saw her brain working through it. She probably was thinking about all the people he knew and who would let him come over or who he would actually call for a place to stay. He saw the moment when it all clicked.

Her face scrunched up. Her lips pulled back. "Oh you didn't! Please tell me you didn't. Hanni? You slept with Hanni?" Her body twisted like something nasty was all over her. "I think I'm going to be sick."

"Oh stop it, Chrys."

"You're the one that put your dick in that fucking skank. She's a walking petri dish."

Spencer shook his head. "She's not like that."

Chrys' fingers plowed through her hair. "She's a drug addict, Spence."

He put his hands in his coat pockets. They were instantly cool from the dampness. He knew she was right. Hanni had been a party girl since before she came to work at the restaurant. He had seen her with a few men who were not on the best side of the tracks. But his sous chef also stepped on that side from time to time. And Spencer was no saint. "She's not a drug addict. She got wasted that one time and -"

"The one time that she OD'd and we had to save her life? *That* one time? Haven't you noticed her sniffing all the time? She's a coke fiend."

"She is not." Spencer bit his bottom lip. Time to change the subject and get it away from him. "Should we talk about your boss? What's worse? A guy who has probably had," he took a quick look around and lowered his voice, "Hundreds of people killed just for shits and giggles or a woman who does a little coke now and then?"

"And the hundreds of guys she bangs?"

"You're not that far behind her, Chrys."

"Fuck you!" That was enough to get her back in the car. She slammed the door shut and almost instantly the limousine rolled away.

Spencer looked at the faces of the people around him. They were sad now that the Siblings Alcrest show was over and had to go back to watching the police and crime lab working at what seemed like a snail's pace.

He had to figure out how to get his fish and get home. He needed a drink. The last thing he wanted to think about was who the body parts belonged to, but that was really what dominated his thoughts.

Chapter 10

We're all safe in our homes. We walk in, flip on the lights, close the door and turn the lock. Click. For just a millisecond you have a, "What if," thought, but that disappears like campfire smoke in a breeze. You're in your home. It's safe. What could possibly happen to you there? You have your television to entertain you, your phone to call out, your Internet to distract you, your food to fill you, your clothes to keep you warm and your ginger kitten to cuddle with. It's all yours and you are safe. Nobody ever thinks about the guy sitting in the back seat of the mini-van out front. Nobody cares if he's in there with his shoes off and legs up relaxing behind tinted windows. And nobody sees him drape his arm over the back of the seat and softly caress the hair of the dead woman with one and a half legs.

I'm finding it harder to control my laughter these days. The screams. The pain. Poor Darcy didn't even know what she was doing. Not until she was almost finished with her own leg. Then came the real screaming.

I sit still as headlights brighten the inside of my vehicle. I know I'm safe. I tested the tinting of the windows. You can't be too careful you know. There's all types of strange people out there.

It's a truck. I've seen it before. The lion ready to pounce. The lion behind the wheel.

I watched him earlier commanding his troops. He liked being in a charge. He gave orders and was followed. He wouldn't scream.

The screamer was there and I smiled at her. Her eyes passed over me as if it was only an empty chair on the other side of the bar. I was grey and blended into the background. She'd see me soon enough. Joey was fun. Darcy was decadent. Hanni is going to be amazing. But she won't be next. You have to build up to the finale.

There are others to come first.

I follow the lion with my eyes. Which one of us is the hunter? We're hunting for two different things from the same prey. Or are we? We are both looking for satisfaction. And unlike Mick Jagger we will both get it.

The lion wasn't the first man to visit since she got home. Another came just fifteen minutes ago. A salesman of sorts. He knocked on the door, handed over a package and was given an envelope. I know his type. I've seen him before. What did he deliver? Emeralds, snow balls, a pocket full of green? What was her pleasure tonight? So much to learn about her before we get together. I'll take my time with this one. She must be wooed.

I lift Darcy up by the hair so I can look her in the eye. "What do you think it is?" We both look back to the door as the lion is pulled in by his weapon. I turn back to Darcy and flick my tongue out at her nose touching it and making it swing. It's just a head with skin and fibers hanging down. She's missing some teeth, but she was like that before I came along, and one milky eye sways on her cheek, dangling by the fine chords. Viscus fluid sticks to her skin. Yes, I did that. It makes me laugh. "You're right, Darcy Vaughn, I think she's a snowflake too."

What I do is a learned trade. You can't get this from a text book. Maybe some YouTube pages since there are a lot of sick fucks out there. But to really learn it you have to go out and do it. Hands on. Trial and error.

And you start small at first like learning to not be seen. It sounds cliché, but you first learn to stand outside looking in. Like looking through this window at the lion with his back against a wall and the prey down on her knees in front of him bobbing away on his throbbing member. That's what the cheesy romance books called it.

I left Darcy in the van, but she may have to do that after. She'll need my help.

After looking and being silent is entering. Smelling. Touching. Tasting. Killing.

Perhaps with the right teacher you can be taught certain things, but the joy of it is what comes natural. You have to love what you do. I was taught many things in my life. My father taught me to hunt and fish. School teachers taught me to read. Mom taught me to do what the prey is letting the lion do right now, but I had to watch her with many predators to find that out. That was after she taught me about plants. Mother has taught me a lot.

The lion's on top of her now. How many times was the couch used for that? These two are so pretty. Perfect naked bodies glistening with sweat. One thrusting in the other. I hate them for being pretty.

He has scars. Did he scream when he got those?

Her mouth is open, moaning, calling for God. But can he make her scream? Man or God?

I learned that. I learned how to make them all scream. He taught me and then I perfected it. He taught me all I needed to know to get that satisfaction. He taught me how to make them scream and I learned how to make them do what they'd never think of.

And then he taught me how to hang the chimes.

Chapter 11

"Spencer's just a fucking tyrant. I don't get him anymore. He's drinking at work and being a royal dick to everyone. Half the staff is ready to walk. And he's stopped scheduling me. I've only worked once this week since he found out I work for O'Donnell and that's because Jessie called me and it was last minute. It's been four days since he found the body parts in his truck and he still hasn't really talked to me. How long is he going to be a dick?"

Sloane was so glad it was dark in the car and Chrys couldn't see the faces she was making. This was the fourth night in a row she went on about her brother the tyrant dictator with a God-complex. Sloane was tired of hearing about it. That and she didn't care anymore. "Have you tried talking to him?"

"No."

"Why not?"

"Screw him, that's why. Turn right."

Sloane signaled and made the turn. "You have to talk to him, Chrys."

Chrys groaned. Her eyes moved from searching the sidewalks to looking at her phone. She was waiting for the next Tweet with #Middletonclown attached to it. She found a small community of people looking for the creepy clown every night. They patrolled the city streets looking for him trying to get pictures or video with him. The nights Chrys didn't drag her girlfriend out were the ones everyone seemed to spot him. Last night he had been seen in High-end pulling a little red wagon. She missed finding him and wasn't happy.

"Did I tell you what Spence said to me at the fish market?"

"Yes, Chrys, you told me a dozen times. And a dozen times you told me how you weren't going to listen to him. I'm good to have a gander for this clown, but I ain't listening to you complain 'bout Spencer anymore."

"Fine." Chrys stared out the window at the city. It was very modern with a touch of old-school class. She liked the fact that it was always changing and evolving. New buildings were going up and old ones were being taken down. Down by where she worked it hadn't changed much in thirty years. They crossed a street and Chrys saw the main downtown. The giant skyscrapers were brightly lit. There was a large crane above the skeleton of a new building going up. She liked the downtown ... from far away. Chrys turned to Sloane. "Did I tell you about the second victim?"

Sigh. "Go ahead."

"Her name is Darcy Vaughn. She worked as a prostitute on Hastings. She was seventeen, had run away from home at fifteen and had been arrested for prostitution and drug possession. Because she was under age she always got let off easy. She got sent home, but would be gone soon after and from what I'm told her mother didn't really care. Emerald was her drug of choice." Chrys cringed. The drug Emerald was a pale green rock crystal. Basically methamphetamine. Potent. Deadly. She and her brother almost got killed over the new drug that was ruining lives all over the province. She still had the bullet scar on her arm. "The coroner's report said her limbs were cut with a handsaw. The cuts were very jagged and rough and the ends had been cauterized as if seared with hot metal."

"Seriously?"

"They think she was alive when some of her limbs were cut off. The coroner said there is a chance that by the angles Darcy may have cut off her own leg. Sick, right?"

"How would you even do that?"

Chrys couldn't control her smile at the look of disgust on Sloane's face. "That's what his report said. The cut was made at such an angle that it may have been self-inflicted."

"How do you know all of this?"

"Turn right." Chrys had a plan. She wasn't certain how well it would go over with anyone involved. "Liam has friends on the Middleton police force. He got the reports and passed them on."

"Really, Chrys? I haven't been in this city a long time, but I know ya don't want to mess with Liam O'Donnell. He's notorious, isn't he? Working for him is one thing, but this may be crossing the line."

Chrys didn't say a word. She was tired of people telling her what she should or shouldn't do or who she could work for. She wasn't doing anything illegal. Her eyes and ears were open at work. The moment she saw anything wrong she had plans to walk. She could walk away whenever she wanted to. Like an addict, she almost believed it.

"Pull over up here."

It took a moment for Sloane to realize what part of the city they were in. "No, Chrys. You can't be serious."

"We might find the clown here. Nobodies spotted him yet tonight."

The street they were on was teaming with life considering it was past midnight. The sidewalks were crowded with a wide variety of people. In other parts of the city it was all quiet with everything locked up and people sleeping and getting ready for tomorrow. Here on Hastings Street the world was alive. The Finish Line had tables out on the sidewalk with a fence around them and a big bouncer not letting any drinks out of the sports bar. Customers were spilling out. Music thumped from another bar. Dean's Diner, with its 24 hour breakfast was doing better than The Alcrest on most nights. A few small stores were open selling random items like hemp products, alcohol and food. The tourist trade was surprisingly good here. People were taking pictures and enjoying the scene. In a few weeks when the welfare checks came out the busiest people around would be paramedics, firemen and police as the calls for overdoses came in.

Prostitutes hung out in groups close to the curbs on both sides of the street. As cars pulled up or got close the ladies would step forward and talk to whoever was inside. Chrys was surprised to see such an illegal act so out in the open. Some of the girls propositioned people walking down the street. And it wasn't just female prostitutes either. Women and men were dressed in skin tight or barely there clothing waiting for someone to pay them for their bodies.

The air smelled skunky. It was like a wild skunk had sprayed a block away and the wind carried it. The glorious stench of marijuana. Welcome to British Columbia.

"What are we doing here, Chrys?"

Chrys' eyes were wide looking at all of the sights. When she was a teenager it was a Friday night thing to drive down the street yelling out the windows at the hookers. Seeing what some of the women were wearing she absently thought Hanni would be right at home. "Darcy Vaughn worked down here. Maybe I can find someone who knew her." She saw a man and woman get close to each other and do a not so subtle slight-of-hand making her wonder if she could find someone who knew Joey Love too.

"What's Spencer gonna say?"

"Why does everyone always ask me that? Who cares what he says? He doesn't want anything to do with me or this and I don't need him. Whoever killed Joey Love and Darcy Vaughn obviously has something to do with Spence, whether he wants to see it or not. Either you're with me or you're against me."

"Calm down, Sweetheart. I only don't want you to fight with your family. I'm with you." The Australian looked tougher than Chrys did and she was glad she was along.

It took them asking eight people before finding someone who knew the name Darcy Vaughn. Number nine was a dark skinned woman with bright pink lips and copper toned hair cascading over bare shoulders. Her tube-top and skirt were the same cheetah print. The bottoms barely kept anything hidden and the top busted out. Her belly sat over the skirt. She also wore chunky high heels that had her almost as tall as Chrys. She was your cliché version of a street hooker smacking gum and yelling to get people's attention.

"D'you mean young blond Darcy or old grey Darcy? Cause old grey Darcy's been gone two years now at least."

"Young one, I guess. Darcy Vaughn. She was seventeen." Chrys watched the woman who said her name was Diamond. She was glad she felt Sloane right behind her.

"That must be young blond Darcy. Not everyone down here is fond of last names. Some not even first names." She had a diamond tattooed on the side of her neck. "Why're you looking for little Darcy?"

"I just want to find out what her life was like."

"Was? You keep saying was."

Darcy Vaughn was under the age of eighteen, so legally the police couldn't release her name to the press without the parent's consent, so maybe they weren't telling anyone. Chrys was going to either lie or get herself into possible trouble. She wasn't new to trouble.

"She was found dead a few days ago. I want to see if I can find out what happened to her."

"Dead? Explains why I haven't seen her in a couple weeks. Thought she might have moved on to another corner. We tend to do that too. Darcy had that Julia Roberts fantasy about being down here. She thought some rich guy would come down and whisk her away in his white limo. The only time we get a limo down here is some ugly fat rich prick wants a bj that only lasts to the next block. And Darcy was no Julia Roberts. She had tiny baby titties and a white girl's ass. No offence."

Sloane smiled. "I'm Australian, mate. I've got ample booty."

"Yes you do. You both do. Maybe you're both a little black."

Chrys couldn't resist the perfect moment. "Oh, believe me, I've had a little black in me once or twice."

Diamond flashed them a huge smile. One tooth was grey. "I like you. Darcy was no movie star hooker. Especially not using Emerald like she did. That shit can fuck you up. When she wasn't sick she was all paranoid thinking someone was out to get her. I guess maybe they were."

"Do you remember when you last saw Darcy?"

"No." Diamond lit a hand rolled cigarette. It might not have been tobacco. "One day blends into the next."

"What about Joey Love? Do you know that name?"

"Don't think so."

Chrys was running out of things to ask. "Do you know who Darcy got her drugs from?"

"Pick one." Diamond waved her hand out. "Every second person down here is holding or selling something. Here comes one of my regulars. You keep asking around and tell people Diamond says you're okay." She strutted off toward an old pick-up which had pulled up to the curb.

Not many wanted to talk to the two women, even with Diamond's name. Darcy was a nice girl in over her head. Probably all she had to do was call her parents, say she wanted to go home and she would have been saved. Maybe not. She had arrived on Hastings a few months ago and struggled to make it through the end of winter. She did what she felt she had to and she had that craving for a drug that would never end.

Joey Love, on the other hand, was a shadow. People said the name sounded familiar, but nobody knew who he was. He probably lost himself for hours or days without knowing anything until the poison wore off. Another lost boy trying to find himself in the drugs.

Both Darcy and Joey were high risk targets. They were willing to go off with complete strangers, few questions asked. Darcy probably got into many cars and was whisked off to who knows where with some strange man. Chrys looked around at the prostitutes up and down the street wondering how they could do it. They just went and gave themselves to strangers. She was often told she was fearless, but these women were the true definition of the word – no matter how illegal their careers were. They were targets just standing there waiting to be picked off. Both of them, all of them, were just there waiting to be taken and cut into pieces.

A shiver ran down Chrys' spine. She felt like she was being watched. As she looked around she realized dozens of eyes were on the two of them. And there were probably a dozen more she couldn't see. It was a place where witnesses were all over the place, yet nobody saw anything.

Chapter 12

"Okay, everyone," it was thirty minutes before the hopeful dinner rush. Spencer hated addressing everyone before service, but he needed them all to be on their game. They were all in the dishpit. The three cooks stood in one corner (Gordie itching to get outside for his pre-service smoke) and the servers were spread out. Wylie would tend bar, Chrys stood next to Izzy and Hanni was close to the chef. Spencer didn't really want his sister working, but Sue asked for the night off and Dee defected to Legend. "Tonight should be a good night. We have a few reservations and with Jimmy Gregor playing I expect a good crowd. Try your best to get everyone on three courses. Let's be the best restaurant in town tonight." He felt so stupid.

As everyone scattered Chrys tried getting her brother's attention. She wanted to tell him everything she found out last night.

Spencer never raised his eyes to look at her as he walked past.

"Everything ready?" Spencer stepped into the hotline. All of their prep had been done an hour ago. Ranger was pulling tongs down from the hanging rack and sticking them over the handles of the oven. Mallory had her mixing bowls and tongs ready. Spencer checked that he had clean rags in his cubby hole under the pass. Hanni had put a drink there for him already.

"Yes, Chef."

Jimmy Gregor was a local country singer with a good following, so by all accounts it should have been a good night. The only reason he was playing at The Alcrest was that he and Spencer had known each other in school.

"Spence, we need to talk." Chrys took her place across the pass. She kept her hand on her billfold.

Spencer moaned. "No we don't." He smiled at a couple that walked in the front door. As Jessie led them to a table he nodded to her and pointed at his sister. "You have a table." He turned his back to her and tapped the stovetop with a set of tongs.

"You're such a dick." By the time Chrys was at her table she had a smile on her face and was her cheerful self. She could be professional. Didn't mean while she was getting the couples drinks she wasn't constantly looking at her brother hoping to flip him the bird. No such luck. She had to settle for, "Order in, your Highness Sir."

Spencer snatched the piece of paper. "Do you want to grow up?"

"Do you want to not be an ass? Like seriously, what the fuck's wrong with you lately? You've been yelling at everyone. Nobody likes you right now."

"Okay guys," Jessie was suddenly there beside Chrys. She grabbed the woman's arm and stared at Spencer. "You can talk about this after we close. Okay?"

Spencer dropped his eyes to the order chit from Chrys. "Order in. Scallop ceviche, Alcrest salad. Second course; New York strip well done, chicken Alfredo."

Mallory repeated the cold appetizers as she was already making them.

Gordie replied with, "Strip murdered and mutilated."

"Just repeat it as called," Spencer snapped.

"See, he's a dick," Chrys said to Jessie loud enough so that her brother could hear.

"Chrys, save it for later. We'll talk about it after work, I said." Jessie herded Chrys away. She looked at Spencer, but his back was turned. The last thing they needed was the two Alcrest's going at each other with customers around. It was going to come to head sooner or later, but hopefully not while the restaurant was open.

Chapter 13

People don't notice normal or average at events. You put a juggler in the center of a crowd and nobody sees the pickpocket cleaning up on the outside. Not until it's time to drop a tip.

You put a man on a stage in a full room and all eyes go on him. If you're looking straight ahead you can't see what's in the corner. Nobody sees who's watching them watching the man on stage. I showed up late, ate my salad and halibut (highly recommend it and the spicy pecans on the salad should be sold by the bag) and now I leave when the crowd is getting large.

They don't see me get up from my corner table and pass through them. The chef nods at me. The woman I seek doesn't even notice I'm there as I brush by close enough to smell her. I'm not someone she would look at normally. I'm nobody. I'm not like the lion or the pretty boy up on stage. She'd notice them. She doesn't even see me. And she served me my food.

Nobody in this room sees me. I could walk up behind any person in the restaurant and end their life with a simple flick of a blade. Just a slice of a throat. Hot blood pouring out over my hand and down their chest soaking through their clothes. Splatter across the table. People would scream. They'd start to scatter away from the bloody mess rushing toward the door. Nobody here realizes how unsafe they are at this very moment. At any moment! Anyone could be killed for no reason at all. I could take the powder from my pocket and play my game. I'm the hunter with all the power and they don't see me.

It's giving me a boner.

You have to pick the right time to move. If you make sure everyone is busy they won't even see you drop an envelope on the hostess stand.

Oh look who's here.

Chapter 14

Jessie came from the hallway and smiled at the two women that just walked through the front door to the restaurant. At first glance they seemed to be opposites. One was fancied up and other more natural. Both had a similarity to them, however. "Welcome to the Alcrest. Do you have a reservation?"

The one with the ironed straight blond hair said, "Spencer said he would save us a table. Washburn."

Jessie moved a small white envelope off the reservation book. She picked up a couple of menus.

"Could we sit in Chrys' section?" Detective Washburn's thin red lips formed into an impish grin. No harm in playing with the girl who was putting her nose where it didn't belong.

The restaurant was bustling. It was busier than Spencer had hoped. The singer had gone on at 7:00 pm and had been playing for almost two hours. Jimmy Gregor was handsome with a rugged look to his face and thick arms, plus his voice was soothing and his songs full of love and meaning. The tables were a third taken, mostly with women, and the orders continued to roll in. They were actually turning over tables and putting in a second seating. The ones that were staying for the entire show were on another round of appetizers and drinks. Soon the singer would be done and people would slowly file out. Hopefully they would buy dessert first.

Spencer looked up as the women walked by.

"Come see me when you have a moment," the detective said and gave him a smile. She didn't look as threatening as she was at crime scenes. She was feminine soft.

Spencer gave her a nod then returned the, "Good night," to a man on his way out.

Jessie led the two women to a far table near the frame room. "Have a seat, ladies. Chrys will be right with you." On her way back she twisted around tables until she was beside Hanni. She had to speak so close to the woman's ear that her lips almost touched it. "Someone left an envelope for you at the hostess stand."

"What is it?"

"I don't know. It was there when I came back from the dishpit."

Hanni went to the bar and got drinks for table eight. As soon as she put them down and gave the customers a wink she made her way to the hostess stand. She picked up the small letter size envelope and found that it had a lump in it. Written in pen on the front was: To Hanni, my favorite waitress. She cringed at the word waitress, but was always willing to accept gifts.

"What's that?" Chrys was returning to the dining room after dropping off dirty plates in the back.

"A gift from a satisfied customer." Hanni flashed white teeth.

"I thought they usually left it on the nightstand."

Hanni's smile turned upside-down. "Funny. You have a new table. Enjoy."

Chrys looked across the kitchen, her face ready to twitch in pain if her brother looked her way, but she couldn't see through the bar area to the new table. Most of her tables were on main courses and yes, she was playing up the desserts. That should please her brother for a second or two. She watched the man in tight jeans and a muscle bulged T-shirt on the stage as she walked in front of the pass. He was coming to an end soon. She wondered if Hanni had tried replacing Spencer yet. Chrys' gaze fell on the new table and she almost stopped. This wasn't going to be great.

"Good evening, Detective Washburn."

"You can call me Wash. This is my sister, Moose."

"Moose?"

The other woman flipped thick waves of dirty-blond hair over her shoulder. She had a very Bohemian look. "Childhood nickname that I never shook. Can I get a Latin Lover?"

Wash said, "I'll have a Coors Light, please."

Chrys returned to the bar and put the order in with Wylie. Hanni was across the room with her envelope. Spencer took off his apron and tossed it into the corner of the butcher's-block. Where was he going? He left the kitchen and walked along the front of the bar. He didn't look once in her direction as he continued past.

As she turned around with the drinks she saw him talking to Wash. Chrys suddenly felt nervous. "Here are your drinks, ladies. Have you had a chance to look at the menu?" Two could play Spencer's game. She could ignore him as long as he could her.

"Not yet, Chrys. I was just going to tell Spencer about this woman who's been asking questions late at night down on Hastings. Dangerous place to be for a curious lady." Her gaze was intense.

Chrys fought back by staring right at her. "It's not so dangerous if the lady had a friend with her."

"Sloane?" Spencer actually looked at his sister. She couldn't help herself and she was going to get someone killed. "How could you take Sloane down there? Do you care about anyone other than yourself?"

"Oh look who's fucking talking, Spence."

"What's that supposed to mean?"

"You've been so focused on your own urges you haven't been bothered to look around."

"Hey, you two," Wash rapped her hand on the table. "Focus. Holy crap, you two need therapy." She pointed a finger at Chrys. "Stay out of my investigation or I'll arrest you."

"Did you get the ViCLAS results yet?" Chrys held her breath. O'Donnell said his source heard the detective went onto the Violent Crime Linkage Analysis System database to see if there had been any other crimes across the country with similar circumstances. It took time to input everything and then you had to wait for the results. Chrys had researched the database set up by the Royal Canadian Mounted Police so that she knew more about it. Mentioning it was probably not a smart thing to do.

Wash drummed her fingers on the table. "How did … Who's your source?"

"What source?"

"You're working on obstruction charges." Wash stopped herself before using words she knew she shouldn't. "I want to know who your source is."

This wasn't what Chrys wanted. She just wanted to make the point that she knew more than the detective thought she did. She felt her brother's burning gaze. She had to think of something. "If I tell you my source, will you tell me what you found out?"

"This isn't a negotiation. I know your source has something to do with Liam O'Donnell. I'm not some dumb blond fresh off the farm. I want to know who his man is in the police department." Wash stared up at her.

Chrys knew there was a way she could get her brother to help. "Tell me what you found out and I'll get Mr. O'Donnell's source."

"No way!" Spencer tried stepping in front of his sister.

Chrys bit her bottom lip to hide a smile and put her arm out stopping him.

"Her life would be on the line if she did that. She's not going against him."

The police detective was thinking about it. What was more important to her? Would anything she told this pain in the ass screw up her case? How important was it to find the mole? She raised a finger and beckoned the server closer. "You tell anyone what I tell you and you'll never cross a street without getting a fine."

"Of course."

"Are you serious?" Spencer growled.

Moose tapped the menu. "Are we going to eat?"

Wash raised a hand, palm up, and curled one finger in a "come hither" motion. She waited until Chrys was close enough that she could smell her minty breath. "Augustus Ryder."

"Who's that? A suspect? You have a suspect?"

"The closest link to this case was an old one from the late seventies. It isn't well known because of other killers like Ted Bundy and BTK that got headlines around the same time. Google him."

"What? So the only thing you got from the criminal database was a case from forty years ago? I have to risk my life for a Google search?"

Spencer had a smirk across his face. He rested one elbow on a hand and used the other to keep his expression hidden. His sister was just railroaded into divulging a mobster's police contact for nothing. He didn't want her to risk her life, but maybe she learned a lesson. At least she was in the hot seat now.

He glanced back at the kitchen. Gordie was moving around fast.

"Augustus Ryder, killed several hookers and dismembered them. He made actual wind chimes out of his victim's fingers and hung them from the trees around his home. That enough for you?"

To be honest, Chrys wasn't happy. She looked at Spencer. He swiftly took off toward the kitchen. She turned back to the two women and said, "Do I have a choice?"

"Not really."

"You can take our order," Moose added in.

What Spencer saw from across the room was his sous chef dropping a plate and his other cooks looking like they were lost. There weren't many tables left to cook for. How could they be screwing things up? He put his hand up to

Hanni as he quickly walked past her stopping anything she was going to say. He stepped through the threshold into the kitchen and found Gordie straddling an upside down plate. The steak was beside one foot and the potatoes and vegetables had sunk into the holes of the rubber mat beneath his feet. His hands quickly moved, but didn't really do anything. "What the hell's going on?"

"Ah," Gordie's head moved toward the boss but he didn't look over his shoulder. "We dropped a plate. I'm re-firing a steak."

"We dropped it?" Spencer stared at the small cook hiding behind the sous chef. "What about the rest of the order?"

"I got this. Don't worry." Gordie had a steak on the grill with a metal weight on top of it, which would push the beef against the hot grill cooking it deeper and faster. It would also push all the natural juices out of it.

"Where's the rest of the order? Where is it?" Even Spencer could hear the anger in his voice. He couldn't stop it. There were three other plates under the heat lamps. Food died under the lamps and food didn't go to the tables in The Alcrest unless the whole table was ready. Three people were going to get dead food and the fourth would get a squished steak with no tasty juices inside. Might as well be at a diner. "Here." Spencer slammed one of the plates on the butchers-block. "Here." The second plate was slammed onto the first. The third followed. Spencer picked them up and almost threw them at Ranger. "Get these the fuck out of here. Where's the order chit? Where is it? Jesus Christ, look at this mess. I leave for ten minutes and you guys fuck everything up."

103

"Spencer! Look at what you're doing." Chrys stood across the pass. Hanni was behind her. Beyond them customers were staring at the kitchen.

"This is my kitchen, Chrys."

"But look at Ranger!" Chrys threw her hand out so fast she sent the heat lamp swinging. "You spilled food all over him," she shrieked. "Who the fuck are you?"

Spencer had been yelling louder than he ever had before. He looked around at all the eyes looking at him. Some showed concern. Some were afraid. Even the police detective was looking in his direction. Mallory stood behind her cold-side table between the kitchen and bar with her eyes down and hands busily making silent work. As Spencer looked at his other cooks he saw what he had done. The only part of Gordie that moved was his arm as he checked the steak. His apron was covered in grease and grime from the busy night. There were mashed potatoes on his shoes.

Behind him was Ranger. He looked down at the floor, the brim of his hat hiding his eyes. In both hands he held the plates close to him. Brown sauce and mashed potato ran down the front of his apron where the plates had tipped when they were shoved at him. Fettuccini hung down beneath them like a chorus of snakes. On cue a dollop of Alfredo sauce dropped from the plates splattering over the twenty year olds shoe.

Spencer looked up from Ranger and caught Jessie's expression just before she turned away. In her face he saw fear.

"Um, let's just redo these plates. You okay, Ranger?"

"Y-yeah, I'm okay."

"Take those to the back and then take a break."
Spencer's voice shook. His arms trembled.

Ranger headed toward the back without a look up at his boss.

Those left in the kitchen went back to work, perhaps a little slower than usual, preparing the previous order. Spencer stayed quiet except for dealing with the orders. As soon as Ranger returned Spencer excused himself and went to his office in the back. For the first time in a while he shut the door closing everyone out.

Chapter 15

Chrys stumbled from her bedroom into the hallway. She loved staying at Sloane's, loved cuddling with her and sleeping next to her and all that fun stuff, but something about sleeping in her own bed all alone was so rapturous.

"What the hell happened to your hair?"

"Fuck you. I'm proud of my bedhead." Chrys' hair was in a mountain of tangles that shot out in all directions. Brushing it out was going to hurt. Her nose caught the scent of something good. Her brother was cooking. She couldn't remember the last time he did that upstairs. Their meals were usually leftover plates from downstairs sealed in plastic wrap or stuff out of a box. "What are you doing?"

Both dogs sat at the edge of the kitchen and took turns looking between her and Spencer.

"Making crepes. You want some? I also made a blueberry compote and orange scented chantile cream. There's coffee made."

Chrys stopped with her bare feet half on the tile floor. The time on the stove clock said it was almost 9:00 am. Even for a Sunday Spencer should have been in the restaurant. "What the fuck's going on? Why aren't you downstairs?"

"I'm taking the day off. I talked to Jessie after work last night and this is the best we came up with."

There was a knock on the door.

Chrys said she would get it and headed across the open room. Her bare feet padded on the floor. Breeze made figure eights around her feet. She liked the idea of her brother taking the day off. The dude needed to relax. And she needed a ride to work on her latest plan. As she reached the door she expected Jessie. It wasn't Jessie.

"What the hell are you doing here?"

"Spencer invited me for breakfast." Hanni sidestepped around Chrys and strutted toward the kitchen.

"Why the hell would you do that?" Chrys yelled from across the room and slammed the door to emphasize her point.

"Because I'm going crazy downstairs." Spencer pulled the fry pan off the heat, wiggled it right then left before giving it a quick twitch with his wrist. The crepe leapt from the non-stick pan, turned in the air and landed perfectly back in the pan with the cooked side up. "I totally lost it last night. You're right. I've been out of control."

"No shit! But why is she here?" Chrys snarled at the blonde's under-bum visible under her Daisy Duke booty-shorts when she climbed onto one of the stools around the kitchen island. Chrys got right beside her brother and whispered a question about Jessie.

Spencer slid the crepe from the pan to a pile of cooked ones on a plate. "This is how I want it to be, Chrys. Are you joining us?"

Time for her to give up. "I'm taking a shower first."

"But you've never looked better," Hanni snickered.

If looks could kill the two of them would have dropped right there. Chrys couldn't help thinking how her brother was just another horny idiot guided by his cock and not his brain. He wasn't supposed to be like that. He was another notch on her bedpost. It wouldn't surprise Chrys if the bitch actually had bedposts or that she was keeping score. She wondered if she graded her lovers by stars or smiley faces.

~ * ~

Freshly showered, dressed in sweat pants and a pink tank-top with her hair tied back and very minimal make-up Chrys bound up to a waiting plate of crepes with a pot lid keeping the heat in. She covered them in chantily cream, syrup and the compote her brother made. As she shoved her first forkful into her mouth she realized it wasn't a plate waiting for her. It was all of the crepes he had made minus what the other two had eaten. Her tongue pushed the food to the side of her mouth, cream clung to the corners. "What are your plans for today?"

Spencer was still standing on the kitchen side of the island leaning against it on his elbows. "Wait and see if my kitchen staff revolts and doesn't show."

"They'll show." Chrys shoveled more sweet food into her mouth. "They love you."

Hanni said, "I wouldn't show if you yelled at me like that." She played with her necklace. It was a pewter sun close to her throat. One of the rays was broken.

Chrys was tempted to look Hanni in the eye and say something about her coming running if someone jiggled the change in their pocket. But that wouldn't be productive. "Gordon Ramsay yelled at his staff and they never quit."

"I'm not Gordon Ramsay."

"True. I have something we can do."

"We?" Hanni sort of snarled at her.

Chrys ignored her. She didn't really mean her anyway. "I want to go check out this place I heard of. It's in the country. Hillsborough."

"Wasn't that where the Creepy House was? This isn't another cistern is it?"

"No." She didn't think so. "It's something different than just being in the restaurant every day and getting pissed off at everyone or hiding up here. Just come with me. I need a ride." Her tongue caught syrup that tried to escape over her lip. She had full lips like Angelina Jolie in Tomb Raider. Sultry, sexy, pillowy lips.

Spencer had to admit going into something where he wasn't in charge sounded good. He hadn't been out of the city since the Fontana Resort thing last summer. "I don't have my truck, remember? It smells of dead people."

They both turned their gaze onto the third person in the room.

"What?" Hanni had barely eaten a thing. She looked at Chrys' plate with an expression of longing. "No. My car's been used in enough of your adventures. I'm not going."

"You don't have to come."

In thirty minutes all three of them were in Hanni's car with Spencer at the wheel and his sister in the backseat. He took the long way to the rural area of Hillsborough instead of taking one of the old-school cable ferries across the river. His last experience with one of those was a memorable one. The fields were sprouting with new buds and trees were a brilliant green. He actually took a deep breath and let his body relax. The restaurant was in the back of his mind, however. If the cooks couldn't handle it he was too far away to get there.

For the first while everyone was quiet, then Chrys realized she had a captive audience and figured that was a good moment to tell Spencer all about her job. By the time she said, "Turn left up here," he knew more than he wanted to about filing shipping requisitions and how Liam O'Donnell liked his coffee.

"Nice necklace, Hanni. Where did you get it?"

"A customer."

Chrys didn't bother asking what Hanni had to do to get it.

They were driving through a wooded area when Chrys finally yelled to pull over. They could see the snowy peaks of the mountains off in the distance behind the trees. The road they were on was paved, though potholes being fixed was a rare thing, with a house or small farm every half kilometer or so. The stretch they stopped on was between two sharp turns. Thick trees lined either side past the deep ditches. The gnarly trees reached out toward the car. It reminded Spencer of a stretch of road he used to bike down when he was a kid. He used to hold his breath and pedal as hard as he could until he was out of the dark stretch. Things were always worse in his mind than they were in reality. He knew better than that now. Reality could be a whole lot worse. Here he was all grown up and his sister insisted on stopping smack dab in the middle of Spooky Forest.

"What are we doing here, Chrys?" Spencer put the car in park, but didn't turn the key. "There's nothing here."

"It should be." Chrys twisted around in the back seat. "I thought I saw an overgrown driveway. Back up."

Spencer put the car in reverse. The engine strained.

"Stop!"

On the right side the ditch had a break in it where a driveway slipped under overhanging trees. The branches had grown so long that they draped down blocking it from sight. In a fantasy movie they would have curled up revealing the gravel path which the hero's must travel. Plants had broken through the packed driveway trying to take it over. Chrys knew this was no fantasy land. This was the Outer Rim and she wanted the others to follow her in. She got out of the car and headed down the old driveway pushing the branches aside before anyone could say anything.

"Chrys, where are we?" Spencer had to stop and wait for Hanni to complain about the bugs before he could follow. He snapped twigs and branches instead of pushing them aside. Still Hanni's bare legs got scratched and she wailed like she had been cut. The last thing he needed was to push a branch aside and have it fly back and hit her. The time on his phone said lunch service would just be starting. "Chrys, where are we?"

Chrys didn't look back and didn't say a word. Her eyes searched ahead looking for what? She didn't have a clue.

"Chrys! What are we doing here?"

Chrys looked over her shoulder. She couldn't remember the last time she saw her brother wearing shorts outside. His white hairy legs were blinding. It was hard to take his anger seriously. "This is Augustus Ryder's home." A branch smacked her cheek. "Cock-fucker!"

"You mean the serial killer from the seventies Wash mentioned? What the hell, Chrys?" He really should have expected this.

"What? I Googled him last night. She told me to, so she was basically telling me to do this. I got the address and found out it was most likely still here from Google-Earth. If they didn't want people to come here they shouldn't have it on Google."

Spencer slapped at a bug that landed on his leg. He ignored Hanni's whines. His sister was the queen of excuses, but blaming this on Google was a new one. "And you don't think Detective Washburn will have something to say about this?"

The covered driveway opened up to a yard which looked like it had not been touched by anything other than wild animals in the forty years since Ryder was arrested for his crimes. There was a wide open yard covered in old grass which had grown so tall it fell over on itself before dying and turning brown. There were patches of hard ground where no grass grew at all. The woods had encroached on the yard. Willow bushes grew all around out buildings as if they were swallowing them up and sprung up through-out the yard. The Alcrest's were getting the sense that they had been to a place much like this before.

"So what happened to Augustus Ryder?" Spencer stared at the two story house in the corner of the yard. It was amongst too many trees to be visible from the road. The blue paint was faded and non-existent in parts where it had peeled off completely. A small sapling grew from collected dead leaves in a rain gutter. There was a roof covered deck that seemed to circle the whole building. Window panes were smashed. The roof itself was shingled, but they were

113

now grey and white curling back. Green moss made strange patterns across the entire roof. Someone had spray-painted something on the walls, but what it had once said was long faded to the point that it was illegible.

Chrys looked from the house to the sheds. She winced at the odour of the place. She knew from Google-Earth that there was a pond behind the buildings. Maybe that was where the foul smell was from. It was a rotten smell. "Police came here and found his finger and toe wind-chimes lining the driveway. He had them all around the house and had more body parts that he tried disposing of in the water over there through those trees. A news report said his wife and teenaged daughter were living here with him."

"Did it smell like this then?" Hanni slapped at bugs real and imaginable. Her nails scratched at every part of bare skin.

"Probably worse."

"You two are so gross."

"Look at the deck," Spencer said and as if on cue the wind picked up and dozens of wind-chimes hanging from the roof began to play their sounds.

There was the tinny sound of metal on metal. A few were hallow pieces of bamboo connecting with a solid block. There were hand-made ones of plastic tubing and hallow pipes. Dozens of different sounds all being made by a simple breeze. It made all three of them freeze in their tracks. The small hairs on their necks stood upright. Goose-flesh erupted over Hanni's body.

"Nobody is here right? The family is long gone, right?" Hanni's voice shook. She wrapped her arms around her body as she felt a chill.

114

"Why would anyone have all those wind-chimes?" Chrys stared at them. "Who likes wind-chimes that much?"

"This is creepy," Hanni said.

Chrys stepped closer to the house keeping her eyes pointed up at the chimes. Any one of them would have made a lovely sound. All of them together was a muddled mess of noise. "Spence, wouldn't the police have taken the wind-chimes as evidence or something? Would they still be here?"

"Evidence of what?" He stared at the shacks behind them. When he was a teen his dad bought houses, usually in the country, to fix them up and resell them at a profit. He and his friends that he had then would have pedaled their bikes for kilometers just to break into old abandoned houses to see what was in them. Maybe find a treasure. Maybe find something they could sell for candy money. He couldn't help wondering what was in those sheds. His friend Jan had always looked for anvils. They were worth money.

"I don't know. He hung his victim's digits up, so maybe these show a pattern or something."

When the breeze came from the direction of the sheds and the pond hitting Spencer in the face he recognized the smell. He started toward the trees.

There was a break in the woods to the right of one shed. The girls stood for a moment listening to the wind-chimes before following. Chrys first and then Hanni because she didn't want to be left alone. As Spencer got closer to the opening he saw an old wood fence pitched at an angle. Beyond that there were dead trees around and inside the lime-green algae covered water of a stagnant pond. The smell could have been a mix of algae and dead vegetation.

115

It could have been an animal that had died. It could have been. He knew it wasn't. He remembered that smell from the cistern. It was damp and rot and something else.

Spencer tested the wood on the fallen fence. Was that a boot print in the mud below it? Did his shoe leave that? He pushed himself up. There was a peaked roof along the side of the pond. He wondered if it was just a roof or if the building had sunk into the slimy water.

"What the hell is that smell?" Hanni yelled out. It made Spencer jump.

"Spencer! Above you!" Chrys pointed at the trees just to his left.

Spencer looked up at the branches above his head. They weren't branches hanging down. Four limbs all hung together from one branch. At first he thought they were moving. The fingers twitched. Then he saw the army of maggots wiggling up and down the rotting flesh. Spencer looked at his shoulder. His hand shot up and dusted away a few maggots that had landed on him. The bits of moving rice disappeared into the ferns covering the ground. He fell back off the fence, his feet stumbling.

A high pitched scream erupted from deep inside Hanni.

"Look awa-" Spencer forgot what he was saying as he saw Hanni. She wasn't looking at the maggot filled limbs.

She was staring the other way at yet another wind-chime. This one had six arms around a central device. The flesh of the limbs had long dried. In the center was a head hanging by long hair tied to a bare poplar branch. It was the solid device that the hollow tubes struck against to create the chime noise. So much of the face was gone that none of them could tell if it was a man or woman. They couldn't tell if it had melted off or was eaten.

116

Hanni's body wrenched forward as the few crepes she had eaten came up and out.

"In the water!" Chrys pointed to something along the edge of the pond. The algae had formed in around it. It was a quarter torso sticking out. The arms were gone, the head missing. They couldn't tell if the legs were still attached because the bottom was below the murky water. A floppy breast floated on the surface. "There's more!"

Like a reveal in a movie their eyes focused on human wind-chimes that spread out around the lagoon. In the water they could see bits of discarded bodies. A breeze seemed to kick in and the hanging limbs and heads all around the pond swung and knocked against each other. No sound came from them. The only sound was Hanni's whimpering and the chimes back at the house. Their songs echoed through the woods and all around them.

"We got to get out of here." Spencer backed away from the pond. He checked his shoulders again. Nothing was there, but he wiped anyway.

"What do you mean? This is awesome."

"You're fucking sick!" Hanni gagged again but nothing came out.

"This isn't awesome, Chrys. You see those maggots? That kill wasn't that old. A week. Maybe." Spencer's voice was desperate. He saw something register in his sister's eyes.

She stared at him. "We have to get out of here."

Birds were singing in the trees. All different kinds of birds. Ravens yelled at them. The wind-chimes at the house still sang. Beyond that they heard the sound of a vehicle engine. It came through the trees like a warning. Something was coming.

117

Spencer's hand went to his left pocket in his shorts. The utility knife he usually had clipped to his pocked at work wasn't there. Why would he need the knife he used to open boxes and packages at work if he wasn't working? That was his thought this morning when he had to decide if he was going to take it.

The engine noise built. It was coming closer and closer. They couldn't tell what direction it was coming from.

"Let's go," Spencer said.

Chrys glared at him hoping he'd understand her thoughts. As far as she was concerned it was the killer coming back. Maybe he had a fresh kill ready to be hung.

The blond hadn't stopped shaking. Her skin had gone whiter than usual and her eyes were glassed over. The phrase, white as a ghost, certainly could have been used to describe her.

Spencer nodded to his sister and flicked his head to Hanni telling Chrys in a silent way to take care of her. He looked to the ground as he headed back toward the house. A two inch thick, three foot long stick was the best he could do.

Chrys put her hand on the back of Hanni's shoulder and pushed her after her brother. She went without a word.

They could tell the engine turned the corner. The driver would see Hanni's car. What would he do? It got louder.

It instantly got quieter as it continued past.

"They didn't stop," Chrys stated. "It wasn't him. Anyone else wet?"

"Jesus, Chrys. Let's get the fuck out of here," Spencer said. He didn't let go of the stick until they were all in the car.

Chapter 16

"What … give … what …"

I slice into my steak setting the blood free. "What did I give you? Is that what you want to know?" The rare steak piece goes in my mouth as I stare at the blank eyes that look back.

"The slang for it is Devil's Breath."

Crystal doesn't move. She sits at the other end of the table just blinking and that is it. In front of her sits a plate with a raw slab of meat almost covering the entire thing. On one side is a fork and the other a steak knife. Her wine sits untouched in a tall glass.

"Pick up your fork, Crystal." I watch her hand come up and grab the utensil. "Now your knife. Eat your meat."

The woman slowly cuts into the raw meat. The flesh tugs at the knife as its teeth tear through the fibers. She lifts the small fork placing the cube of meat in her mouth. It squeaks as her teeth chew away.

Crystal doesn't seem to notice the centerpiece which stares at me. The eyes are foggy, but he can see me.

"Do you know what's funny?" I point at Crystal with my fork. "The drug is called Devil's Breath, but the flowers it's made from are called Angel's Trumpet. Bitter irony I think."

I had learned about the drug a long time ago. It is odorless. Tasteless. And victims of the drug stated it turned them into living zombies devoid of their own free will. They did whatever they were told without question.

"When I walked passed you the other night," I ignore the eyes looking at me and speak to the blank ones of Crystal, "I held up my hand and blew you a kiss."

Hastings was full of its usual scum the night I took Crystal. Men and women walking around looking to make money by selling their bodies, only to return to the same corners to buy poison. I walked through the crowd weaving in and out. Unseen. Nobody noticed me. Nobody saw my hand come from my pocket with white powder in the palm. Nobody but Crystal saw me blow her a kiss – blow the powder in her face. Devil's Breath went into her nose, mouth and eyes. I was the Devil and she took in my breath. It worked fast. "In seconds you were mine and all I had to do was whisper a command into your ear."

"What ... about ..."

"What about you, Stan?" I tap the man strapped to the table on the forehead with my fork. "You're a drug addict. Getting a white powder in your face was easy."

The official police statement on the drug I use – urban myth. The drug is just like me. It isn't real. The bogeyman in powder form.

"How's your meat, Crystal? Sorry I didn't cook it."

120

Crystal goes on cutting pieces off her steak and chewing them without any acknowledgement that anyone else was there.

"How is it?"

She doesn't say a word.

"How is Stan? For an Emerald addict he sure had a lot of meat on him."

The eyes on the table go wide. He's on the edge of his trip. He realizes what is going on, however can't do anything to stop it. This is the best part. The hallucinations in the middle can sometimes be fun, but this is where I enjoy myself. In reported cases about my drug the perpetrators were long gone by this part. This is when they start realizing what is happening to them. This is the part where their minds snap free from reality and you can watch it happen in their eyes.

Stan's body wiggles. Poor stupid bastard doesn't even know that his one arm is cut off at the elbow. He sawed it off with vigor. He cut the piece of meat off of his thigh and put it on Crystal's plate.

"Put down the knife."

Crystal places it carefully beside the plate. Her teeth continue to squeak against Stan.

"Pick up the saw."

Without hesitation her hand moves to the extra utensil. Her fingers flex around the handle of the hacksaw as she lifts it into the air. Her glassy eyes stare at the blade. It is covered is dried blood from the last time it had been used. She is the one who used it to cut off Stan's foot. He screams like a girl.

I lick my lips. This is the fun part. "Start sawing your other arm at the elbow."

The teeth of the blade tear into the skin of the inside of her left elbow without hesitation. Blood splashes out across her side of the table. Her right hand moves back and forth as the tool does its job. The teeth hold bright crimson flesh as it moves back and forth tearing it from her arm.

Stan begins to scream. Blood vessels erupt in the whites of his eyes. Crystal can see the saw's teeth ripping her own limb apart, but she can't stop herself from pushing and pulling the saw. She has to keep cutting until I say stop. Even Stan's screams don't phase her.

I reach under the table and stroke myself. This is the good stuff. As long as she doesn't pass out from blood loss I will finish. I love the screams. Stan's drug trip was over when Crystal cut the flesh off of him. It was erotic.

It's all erotic. Stan's screams, Crystal's blank eyes, the sound of the hacksaw scraping against bone, her hot blood filling the tabletop, the way it squirts out of her upper arm like a teenaged boy playing with himself over and over.

It doesn't matter what they've found.

Grandpa was right. I've read his journals. There is no better feeling than what you get from seeing fear in someone's eyes. I wish he was here to know the sound of their screams. It's far better than those wind-chimes he loved. My wind-chimes don't make a sound. They bring the sound out of others.

Did she scream when she first saw them hanging around the pond? Was it from fear or disgust or knowing that it excited her that made her wail? Did her nipples get hard? I can't wait to find out.

Chapter 17

"Thirty-two."

Spencer put a half teaspoon of sauce to his lips and blew on it. The temperature was still too hot. He let the orange sauce coat his tongue before swallowing.

Wash continued, "At least until the DNA results come in we have thirty-two victims. Some limbs may not belong to torsos and vice versa. Medical examiner estimates some have been there for years and as recent as two weeks before the Leigh Park limbs were hung." She paced back and forth in front of the pass. Every time she turned the closest fingers drummed along the tile top. There were bags under her eyes and her skin had a ting of grey to it. She probably needed a good nights worth of sleep. Being around death couldn't be easy. "There were signs of animal activity, s we may not have all the parts either. We've started a search pattern around the property to see if anything got dragged away."

Chrys leaned on the corner beside the basket of lemons that was always there for a quick garnish or flavor. "Glad we could help."

"Help?" Wash's feet stopped. Her fingers on the pass curled into a fist.

Spencer dropped his tasting spoon into a tin canister of water and sanitizer. He looked at his cooks. "Guys, Mallory, why don't you take a break."

Wash waited until the kitchen staff was gone. The only customer in the restaurant was Mr. O and he sat in his usual spot by the window. "Help? You didn't help. My boss is asking me how the hell you two found out about the Ryder place before me and what the hell you were doing out there."

"We were out for a Sunday drive and stumbled on it. Pure coincidence."

"Oh shut up, Chrys. My boss knows who you are. She's not going to buy that crap. I told her we had a leak in the department and you are going to tell me who that is."

"See, no worries."

Wash's green eyes glared at Chrys. The heat-lamp reflected in her glass lenses. "I want O'Donnell's source at my desk by this time tomorrow or you'll be locked up." Wash was done playing around. "You refuse -"

"Do you want me to get killed?"

"You refuse," Wash repeated, "and I'll arrest you right now. What's O'Donnell going to say with his brand new secretary being paraded around the police station?" A smirk crossed her lips.

"Is this Law & Order or something? Does this shit work in real life? I don't know anything about what O'Donnell does outside of work, so there's nothing for him to worry about. And it's administrative assistant, not secretary." Chrys stuck out her tongue. Yes, it was childish, but at the

124

moment it seemed the right thing to do. Her *resting-bitch face* wasn't doing the trick.

It was Thursday. Four days ago they found the pond and most of its secrets. Since Sunday the Middleton police department and local RCMP had been collecting everything. They drained the pond and found a sickly display of flesh and bone. More body parts had sunk to the bottom of the pond. Wash looked like she hadn't slept since they called her after they drove away from the abandoned house. She had showered at least, but the scent of lilacs did little to hide the stench of rotting corpses.

"I'll get the source," Spencer said and gave his sister a look that told her to keep her mouth shut. "Detective, why do you think he hung the body parts in Leigh Park? He's been doing this for years without anyone catching on and then suddenly there's a body in a city park and we find his stash."

"I found his stash," Chrys said.

Spencer let out a sigh. "Whatever. Doesn't it seem strange that he would put those body parts in the park?"

Wash checked her watch before looking at each one of them. "Everything seems strange, but leave it to us to get the answers. My warning still stands. If I don't have the snitch by this time tomorrow I'm arresting Chrys." She walked to the door, placed her hand on it and without turning said, "I shouldn't say this, but in the past week we've had two missing person reports from the Hastings area. Stanley Haul and Crystal Stone. This killer is dangerous. I'm not warning you again to stay out of it."

The kitchen crew returned and slowly walked back down the line.

"Okay," Chrys snapped.

"I'm not kidding," Wash got in the last word before walking out.

Chrys took back her position across the pass and tapped the hot tiles with her thumb ring. "Now what do I do?"

"Go teach your dance class." Spencer gave his station a quick wipe down. "Leave the detective work to the detectives."

"But I don't know this detective. How do I know she can do her job?"

"I'm sure Wash is good at her job. She wouldn't be where she is otherwise. I talked to Constable Wright about her. She's had a great career."

"How do I know that? I never saw her before this and since she's come along there are now thirty-five open homicides and a serial killer terrorizing the city. Oh and a midnight clown."

"Just go teach your dance class, Chrys. And you better tell Wash who the source is that O'Donnell has."

"Like I even know. And what are you going to do?"

"Cook." He had other plans in mind, but she didn't need to know.

Chrys had her own plans that she wasn't sharing.

Chapter 18

Five minutes after Chrys left the restaurant Spencer went to his office and actually shut the door. He never shut his door and yet here it was shut again. He sat in his chair and picked up the phone. He hated that he didn't have to look up the number to be dialed. He had called Liam O'Donnell more than he wanted to in the past year. A lot more than his sister knew of.

As he put down the phone there was a knock on the door. Jessie poked her head in. "Everything okay?"

"Yeah. Why?"

"I was told your door was closed and people were worried. Everything's okay though?"

Spencer grinned. Since his blow-up on the weekend he had been able to keep his cool in front of employees. He felt like they were all walking on eggshells around him waiting for him to explode. "I'm good. I need a table for Mr. O'Donnell at 8:00 pm. Grab the one in the corner."

"We don't have many reservations anyway. Why is he coming?"

"I need to talk to him about Chrys."

Jessie leaned on the doorframe with her arms crossed in front of her. The sleeves of her black shirt were rolled up to her elbows. A lot of people thought at first glance that she was lesbian. They both knew different. "Spence, she's a big girl. You have to let her live her life. It's her job."

"This isn't about that. There are things out of my control and her job is one of them."

"That's very new age of you."

For a moment neither spoke. Many times they were in those same positions – Spencer sitting at the desk and Jessie leaning on the doorframe – discussing whatever issues were going on at the restaurant. It was far better than him being mad at everyone.

"Are you free Saturday morning?" Spencer's voice was so soft he wasn't sure if Jessie heard him until she pushed away from the doorframe. He quickly added, "I want someone to go to the Farmers' Market with."

Jessie's eyebrow went up. "What about Hanni? Rumor has it you two are an item."

"Rumor, eh?" He knew who was spreading rumors. "She's not really an early morning gal." He saw a change in Jessie's expression. Maybe he should have denied the rumors. "If you're busy or can't that's okay." He gathered papers from the printer and rose to his feet keeping his eyes down.

"How about I let you know?"

Spencer gave her a smile and nod. As he walked past her he handed off the newly printed menus. They printed out new menus every time Spencer changed something. He was getting back to changing up the menu. Both held their breath as their bodies slipped by each other. Spencer didn't want to catch a whiff of her vanilla scented perfume. He fought the urge to run a hand across her hip.

He had not seen Hanni since the day they found the bodies. Every time he called her she said she wasn't in the mood to talk. She was supposed to work tonight but texted Jessie saying she still wasn't ready to come to work. Spencer had his fears about what she might be doing to cope with what she saw. She had been a fan of little white dust in the past. She swore she was off it. He didn't want to think about it. Hanni wasn't always one to tell the truth and was sure this was one of those times.

~ * ~

At exactly 8:00 pm Liam O'Donnell and his man, Mr. McGregor, walked through the door. The bodyguard was in his usual black suit with the mysterious bulge on his left side. O'Donnell wore a grey suite which was much more casual. In a different world he could have been mistaken as a respected attorney or pillar of business. Some knew him as someone who gave back to the community. Most knew him as the center of many criminal investigations. His name made headlines often on both sides. He had been accused of murder more times than anyone could remember. He made sure nothing ever stuck to him, however.

The moment the Irishman walked in the restaurant the air changed. Conversations halted for a moment before being replaced by whispers.

Spencer's staff never asked why the two of them were involved. Even Spencer wasn't certain. He knew it went back to when his father owned the business and he had never asked about it. Now he was falling in his own hole.

"Is this about Chrysanthemum?" O'Donnell asked as Spencer sat down across the table from him fifteen minutes later. The mobster flicked his finger against the glass in front of him. The man was not used to being summoned or having to wait. He was perfectly groomed from his shaved face to perfect sideburns and every hair in place. "I was wondering how long she'd work for me before you put your nose into it."

Spencer glanced toward the bar and kitchen. He had the mobster sitting at the same table a homicide detective had recently eaten at. "This has nothing to do with my sister. I have questions about it, but that's not why I called you."

"Business looks slow."

"We're making do."

O'Donnell took a sip of his drink. "Are you going to get to the point of this, Spencer?"

"I need to know who you have in the homicide department." Spencer looked up from him to Mr. McGregor who constantly scanned the room. The man was always with the mobster. "I need a name."

"How are the ovens I bought you?"

Spencer let out a laugh. His smile brought out his dimples. He knew that comment was coming. "I need that name."

"Don't you think, Spencer -"

"You know what? I call you Mr. O'Donnell. I think you can do me the respect of calling me Mr. Alcrest."

Liam O'Donnell bit his lip hard enough to leave white marks. He was not used to being put in his place. He walked in a room and intimidated without having to say a word. He sighed. "Don't you think that I've done enough for you and your family? You want me to wreck a man's life, his career? Over what? Your sister playing a game?"

"My sister's going to go to prison unless she gives that name to the police." Spencer wasn't paying attention to what was going on in his restaurant. He had faith that his crew had it. "I don't care, Mr. O'Donnell, about what you've done for me. You bought the ovens when I needed them and I've been paying them off when I can. I want the name of that officer."

"I said, you and your family. Have you heard the name Bradshaw?" The Irish mobster's green eyes pierced right into the chef. He always had a little information hidden away.

Spencer nodded. "The head of the drug ring up at Fontana Hot Springs."

"Last summer you two decimated his business. The boyo wanted you dead. There was a contract out on your lives, Mr. Alcrest." He practically spit the name out. The angrier he got, the more his Irish brogue came out. "Both yours and Chrysanthemum's. As long as your sister works for me and I have an interest in ya, they'll leave you be. As soon as I turn my back the targets turn on. Do ya really want that, Mr. Alcrest?"

Spencer didn't know Liam O'Donnell to bluff. Could there really be a contract out on their lives? If anyone would know it would be the man in front of him. He felt a weight pushing down on his shoulders. "Are you threatening me, Mr. O'Donnell?" He tried to play cool, but there was sweat running down his back and it wasn't from the heat of the kitchen.

131

"I think you'd know if that's what was going on."
O'Donnell finished his drink in one gulp. The ice tinked against the glass as he placed it on the table and pushed it away. "I've lost my appetite." As he started to rise Mr. McGregor quickly pulled the chair out.

The sudden move startled Spencer making him flinch. In his mind he pictured the flash of a gun coming out from inside the jacket. He jumped to his feet. The chair almost flipped. "What about the name? You promised Dad."

"Ey, I did promise your Da to look after you. Keep you safe. But you be a man now. Look at all you have and cherish it. I'm thinking that promise is getting rather stretched, Mr. Alcrest."

As O'Donnell moved to step away Spencer reached out and grabbed his arm. He held his breath. Mr. McGregor moved. O'Donnell put his hand out stopping his man and stopped moving himself.

"Let go of me arm."

"Chrys won't ask you for it, so I am. I need that name."

"Sgt. Dan Pratt." As the Chef let go of his arm O'Donnell continued. "I'll take care of Bradshaw, but I think your father's promise has been well kept. You're on your own from now on, Spencer."

Spencer thought of the scene in the movie Cocktail when that same line was said to Tom Cruise. He hugs his girl and returns with, "The only way I want it." Spencer couldn't say that. He couldn't say anything. He stood by the far table watching the two men leave and felt extremely alone.

Chapter 19

"Sloane, listen to this. The Wind-Chime Killer strikes again … question mark. Police continue to investigate the gruesome discovery of what sources say may be over thirty-two separate victims in the Hillsborough area. A source in the police department states body parts were hung by trees just like the wind-chimes on the nearby house. Are you listening to me?"

"Yeah I'm listening."

Chrys continued reading. "The head detective on the case, Detective Washburn, will neither confirm nor deny any connection with the discovery of hanging limbs made in Leigh Park and again at the Waterfront Fish Market. All three discoveries were made by amateur sleuths, Chris … they spelled my name wrong … and Spencer Alcrest who gained fame last year … then it goes on talking about what we did. Oh Spence is going to fucking hate this."

"Which part?"

"They called us amateur sleuths. He'll go bat-shit crazy." Chrys kicked her ankle boots off and curled her feet underneath her on the passenger seat. The two sat in

Sloane's car outside the Elizabeth Frances Dance Studio where they had been since Chrys finished teaching a class a half-hour ago. "What do you want to do?"

Sloane stared down at her phone. She had no tattoos on her innocent charming face, but there was one of a pulse line on her neck right above where one would take her pulse. Just her face alone with her short dark hair could be seen as a stunning woman or a pretty boy. One arm was covered in more tattoos than the other. Chrys' favorite was the pin-up of the comic book character Harley Quinn.

"Tweets are going crazy about the clown tonight," Sloane said. Her Australian accent still gave Chrys butterflies. "Wind Chime Killer and #MiddletonClown arrived at same time #KillerClown #coincidence? #murderer #killer."

"Nobody likes him anymore."

"Middleton Clown is a psycho in disguise #MiddletonClown #evilclown #SawItMovie #JohnWayneGacy. This one says "Stop the #MiddletonClown before he strikes again."

"It really says, John Wayne Gacy?"

Sloane tilted her phone so Chrys could see. "If I was him I'd hang up the clown shoes for a while."

Chrys didn't really think the clown was the killer. That would be too obvious. It was just some way to freak out the city and play a "catch me if you can" game. Only now he could get himself hurt.

She was thinking about all those lost souls that nobody seemed to miss. There had to be some connection to Augustus Ryder. It couldn't be coincidence.

"Here's another article," Chrys was checking on her phone. "The two victims found in the city, Joey Love and a woman whose name is being withheld under the Young Offenders Act (that must be Darcy Vaughn) had both frequented the Hastings area prior to their deaths. This area is well known within the law enforcement community to be heavy with illegal activity such as prostitution and narcotics. Sources suspect that most, if not all of the thirty-two victims will be linked to Hastings.

"Let's go down there," Chrys said. She licked her lips. The game was afoot. "Let's go down to Hastings. Maybe somebody else will talk to me now. We can ask about anyone missing."

"You're not supposed to be doing this. I thought the detective wanted to arrest you."

"I'm not supposed to do a lot of things." Chrys gave Sloane a sideways smile. She hooked her phone up to the car stereo and put on the song Dumb Dog by the all-female band The Wolfe. She joined in singing the song about being your own person.

"You're crackers."

~ * ~

They parked the car near where they had done before, got on the sidewalk and stayed close to each other. It was not as busy as it was the last time. That could have been because it was Thursday night, but the bodies and the beefed up police presence were the main factor. Probably more the later. Chrys glanced at the police squad car across the street. The officers stood by the front of it watching the people on the sidewalk. The killer could be right there. He could be one of the people on the street. The police knew that to be fact, however they didn't have a clue what to do

135

with that knowledge. They didn't know who he was or what he looked like. What were they supposed to do? Wait for someone to be attacked? Wait for someone to yell, "help this guy has a hard-on for wind-chimes?"

"Chrys, look." Sloane tugged on her arm.

"What is … oh my God!"

A window at the diner had almost been completely covered by pictures and signs. Only slivers of light came through around what was there. Missing posters. Pictures with the dates of when they were last seen. Chrys started counting and lost track as her eyes misted over. Not a colour or race was missed. Brown, blue, green, hazel eyes stared out at her frozen in time and lost. They were just like her mother. There one day and then gone. Teenaged girls and boys. Adult women. People were missing them and put their notices up since the body parts were found. Chrys wondered if the ones searching would like to know they were part of the body wind-chimes or if they'd rather have them still be missing.

"Do you think some of what you found is right here?"

Chrys didn't bother answering Sloane. They both knew the answer. Instead she looked at the faces and read the details of each one of them. Did she see any of them? A Lion tattoo on a bicep? A discoloration in the skin? A birthmark on a cheek? A sun necklace?

She stepped closer to the wall. An eighteen year old girl went missing eight days ago. Crystal Stone did not come home in the morning. Her mother and daughter were missing her. This was the one Wash had mentioned. Chrys focused on her picture. A smiling young woman. Blond hair, green eyes. She was missing a tooth. It was what was around her neck that drew Chrys in. A black leather strap with a silver sun pressed against her throat. One ray was broken off.

Hanni.

She looked over the other pictures for the other name Detective Washburn had said. The missing poster for Stanley Haul was in the top corner. It wasn't as well made as Crystal's. He was in his twenties and looked like he had seen better days from the picture.

"Chrys," Sloane was looking at her phone. "They spotted the clown. It reads like a mob is going after him. People keep posting that they are going after him."

Chrys ran a hand through her hair as she looked around them. They were being watched. She just couldn't see where the eyes were. "They're fucking crazy. This killer is smart. Look at all the people he's taken and killed without being detected. He's not going to dress like some shit-assed clown and parade around town. He'd be right here watching people put up their posters and jerking off every time he recognized one."

"Or would he be part of the mob?"

"Shit! Where does it say he is?" Chrys quickly walked toward the car.

Sloane stayed beside her as she checked Twitter. "Outside the Rawlinson Centre. We can be there in twenty minutes if we get the lights."

Chapter 20

Spencer paused to let the automatic door slide open. He had to park away from the emergency doors and ran through the parking lot, avoiding ambulances as one pulled out and another pulled in. He sidestepped around a man going out. The waiting room inside was standing room only. Nurses moved around quickly. Side doors leading to the back opened and closed as hospital personnel went through. Spencer got in line behind five other people. The clock on the wall said it was 3:07 am. Didn't people have anywhere else to go this late on a Thursday night? Or this early on a Friday morning depending on your outlook? There were drunk people, crying kids with stressed out parents, a group of teens looked like gang members – one of them bleeding, police officers stood by a cuffed man.

He couldn't see Chrys or the one who called him, Sloane. Texting them wasn't getting any results.

Another fifteen minutes and he made it to the front of the line.

"Do you have your health card?" The woman behind the desk asked without even looking up. A giant Big Gulp cup sat beside her keyboard.

"I'm not here to see a doctor. I'm here to see Chrys Alcrest."

The receptionist's eyes rolled. He was breaking her rhythm. "And where is he?"

"She. She's here somewhere. I got a call from her girlfriend that she was here."

"Then why not call her back?"

He was getting pretty close to his boiling point. "I tried. Neither of them are answering."

The receptionist sighed before looking over her shoulder. "Shelly, do you know where Chris Alcrest is?"

A nurse stepped out from behind a small wall where they triaged every incoming patient. Green scrubs draped over her rolling body. "She came in with the mob beating."

"Mob beating?" Spencer's eyes darted from one to the other. "What mob beating? Is she okay? Is Sloane okay?"

Shelly raised a hand. "Sir, please calm down."

"I am calm."

"Have a seat in the waiting room and I will check on her status."

That wasn't what he wanted to hear. He found an empty seat between a sleeping drunk and a woman who kept rocking her baby and whispering for her to calm down. He checked what was happening on Facebook. Nothing. Neither Chrys nor Sloane had updated their status, not that they did that often anyway. He flipped through a Chatelaine magazine and found an article on six refreshing summer cocktails. It was last summer's issue. After watching an episode of Night Court on the television up in the corner his eyes started to droop. He knew he should check on his sister, but sleep wasn't letting him.

"Some worried brother you are."

Spencer pushed himself up in his chair. He wiped drool from his cheek. Chrys stood in front of him. There was a bruise on her left cheek and her right wrist had a brace on it. One finger had metal taped around it. Sloane was behind her holding an ice pack to her mouth.

"Can we go?" Chrys snarled.

"What? Yeah." He waited until they were outside. "What the hell happened?"

"We saw on Twitter that people were going after the clown guy. They were blaming him for the wind-chime killings."

"So?"

Chrys ignored him. "I know he's not the killer, so I wanted to stop them. We got to the Rawlinson Centre and they were already on him by that wolf statue out front. There must have been a dozen people surrounding the clown. They backed him up until he was against the statue." The statue was a large bronze of a wolf watching for whatever was coming. It was painted the colours of a timber-wolf. By the time everything was done it was splattered with blood. "They started hitting him. I saw his balloons float up and I had to do something. Sloane and I ran into the crowd and we started pulling people off him. Then they started hitting us. That was when the cops came. Sloane got a fat lip. I got hit in the face and a broken finger and sprained wrist when I punched a guy. The clown guy has all kinds of fractures and such. Last I was told he was in surgery."

"That was really stupid, Chrys."

141

"I couldn't let this guy get killed. He's not the psycho."

"How do I look?" Sloane dropped the ice pack for a second. Her bottom lip had been split and stitched back together. It was fatter than Chrys' naturally full lips.

"Jesus," was the only thing that slipped from Spencer's lips.

They all got into the car Spencer was renting. He still wasn't sure what he was going to do about his truck.

"Do they know who hit you? Are you pressing charges?"

"I don't know. Have you seen Hanni lately? Heard from her?" Chrys sat in the passenger seat.

Spencer started the car and headed for home. He wasn't sure where his sister was going with her questions. "No. No I haven't seen her since Sunday. Why?"

"Have you talked to her?"

"Briefly."

"When?"

"Why? What does she have to do with this?"

Chrys squeezed the bridge of her nose. "I just need to know, okay? You know that necklace she got from a customer? I think it belonged to a victim." She told him about the picture she saw on the diner window.

"That's ridiculous. It's coincidence." At this time of the morning traffic was almost non-existent.

"Then let's go to Hanni's."

Spencer glanced over at his sister as he shook his head. "Look at the time. We're not going there."

Chrys groaned her frustration. "Come on, Spence. Has Hanni ever received any gifts other than phone numbers and night cap invitations? This can't be a coincidence."

"Quit your yelling. I'm not waking her up. It's four in the morning. I'll go see her later today." He signaled and turned onto Pearson. Their street was completely quiet.

It was on the tip of Chrys' tongue to state Hanni could be bits and pieces by the time he got there. She didn't say it. She had to remind herself that she didn't like the woman. She still didn't want to see her hanging from a tree like a grotesque wind-chime and more than that didn't want her brother to be hurt. She would have to wait and see. She didn't have a good feeling about it. This was enough playing around. She had to find out who this guy was before someone she knew got hurt.

Chapter 21

What happens to a play when the director loses grip and everything goes off on its own? I've made a mistake. I wanted people to see what I do, not see me, and I wanted to taste their fear. I wanted to hear them scream. I wanted to let them know that they weren't safe anywhere. I've lost all control. I hate losing control.

I had a place to hang my chimes. They weren't supposed to find that. How did they get there? I made a mistake somewhere and they took my place from me. They don't get to do that. She doesn't get to do that. I'm going to get my scream and have my fun, but they are going to hurt while I do it.

I sat by the window in Hastings and watched people put up their posters about the missing. They knew nothing. They think they've found it all. They think they've found every one of my actors, but they know nothing. I saw the tour guide and her tattooed friend on the street staring at my collection of chimes. I could taste the fear in everyone who looked at it. They knew it could be them on the window. So simple to make them vanish.

Then I followed and watched the two of them get beat down trying to help that clown.

The people think a lazy clown on a street corner working off of peoples basic fears could do the things I've done? I'm the director. I run this play. They haven't seen anything yet.

Then I passed the lion as he was going into the hospital. Again I was not seen. All they have to do is open their eyes and I'll be there.

Does he know what his girlfriend has been up to?

Chapter 22

"Have you called her yet?" Chrys stood across the pass feeling the heat from the lamps on her face. Her brother was slicing leeks. She noticed he looked at the time every few seconds.

"Not yet."

"Aren't you worried about her?"

"Why, are you worried? I thought you hated Hanni."

"Not so much I want to see her cut into pieces and hung from a tree."

The two of them got a little sleep after the hospital. Chrys made Sloane stay over and they fell asleep right away. Spencer's sleep was restless. In less than four hours he was up and took the dogs for a walk before heading to the restaurant. Chrys came down an hour ago and wasn't giving it a rest.

"Aren't you curious about her?" Chrys was oblivious to the half dozen customers in the restaurant. "Her necklace was a victims."

Spencer pointed at her with his knife. "You don't know that."

"Oh my God, Spence."

The front door opened. Both smiled at Jessie as she came in and headed towards the back.

Chrys waited until she was out of sight. "Does Jess know about you two?"

"She does, but there's nothing really to know."

Chrys stared at him for a moment. He nonchalantly went on chopping his vegetables without a care in the world. Prick. "Do you even care about Hanni?"

"Of course I do."

"Then what are you doing? Call her and find out if she's okay."

"You're being hysterical."

"Hey," Jessie leaned on the kitchen's open passageway. "Hanni called me twenty minutes ago. She said she's sick and can't work tonight. I'm going to call Sue in."

Spencer smirked at his sister. "See."

Chrys ignored him. "You actually talked to her, Jess?"

"Yes. She didn't sound too hot. What happened to your face? And your finger?"

Chrys just shook her head.

"And shouldn't you be at your day job?"

"Yeah," Spencer smiled, "Shouldn't you be fire-bombing cars or running numbers or something?"

He got a massive eye roll in return. "Suck my dick, Spence. Can I borrow the car?" She turned to Jessie without getting an answer from her brother. "Can I borrow your car? Can I use someone's car?"

"No limo today?"

"I called in sick, okay?" She folded her arms across her and pouted. "Can I borrow a car or not?

"Take mine." Jessie dug her keys from her pocket.

148

"I need to speak to Detective Washburn." Chrys put her hands on the ledge in front of bullet proof glass. The metal guard on her finger made a thunk noise. Behind the glass was a police officer who decided who got past the lobby of the police station. She tried to put on her best smile.

"And what is this about?"

So many thoughts ran through Chrys' head. Dead girls. Hanging body parts. Her brother's girlfriend getting torn apart. That thought made her feel instantly ill. It was the words, "brother's girlfriend," that did it. To the officer she said, "It's about the Wind-Chime Killer case."

"Your name?"

"Chrys Alcrest."

The officer punched a number into his phone and spoke a few seconds to who Chrys assumed was Wash. She'd swear she heard the detective groan when the officer said her name. As he hung up the phone he said, "She'll be right out."

A minute later a door opened. Wash said, "Nice face. Follow me," without any other greeting.

As Chrys followed through the door her gaze zipped around. Police officers were all over the place. Being around them made her nervous. "I'm not giving you O'Donnell's source. I don't know the name."

"Dan Pratt," Wash said over her shoulder. She had her hair tied in a ponytail. It made her look younger.

"What?"

Wash stopped walking so suddenly the other woman almost crashed into her. She didn't want to look Chrys in the eye. The idea of a dirty cop on her watch made her sick. She said, "Sgt. Dan Pratt resigned this morning effective immediately. The guy was eight months away from retiring with a full pension. Suspicious right? Then your brother called an hour ago and gave me his name." She spun on the ball of her foot and started walking.

Her brother. How did Spencer get the guy's name? He was sticking his nose in her business again. She began to wonder if she still had a job at the docks or if her brother put his nose in there too.

She was lead to the side room housing the homicide department and didn't speak until she was sitting at a desk. "I thought cops weren't supposed to wear heels."

Wash looked down at her shoes. The black heels were too high for police regulations, but they had almost given up warning her about wearing what shoes she liked. "That's in the field. I'm not in the field." There was a pair of shoes under her desk that were more appropriate. Plus she had another pair in the car. She was well prepared. "Now what do you have to tell me?" She locked her fingers together placing them on the desk as she faced Chrys square on. It could have been the location, but her eyes were more intense.

Chrys felt a shiver go down her spine. She corrected her slouched posture. "I want to know if you have any identities into the thirty-two victims yet."

"I don't give you information. That's not how this relationship works."

"But you got the leak, right? That deserves something."

Wash unfolded her hands and sorted papers on her desk. It was about as messy as Chrys' desk down at the docks.

"I'll be sure to give your brother a big sloppy kiss the next time I see him."

Chrys dropped her chin. "Well he does like blonds."

"What was that?"

"Nothing." She had to change tactics. "Have you seen all the missing posters in Hastings?"

"Of course I have."

"Are any of them victims?"

"I'm sure they are victims of something." Wash ignored the younger woman. She flipped pages around.

Chrys bounced against the back of her chair. "Why did you have me come back here?"

Wash' thin lips turned to a wicked smirk. It made her look like she was up to no good. "To see what you were going to say. I was pretty sure you weren't going to tell me anything." She leaned forward and stared right at her. "Stay. The. Hell. Out. Of. This. Do you understand? You're going to get yourself killed. From what I've heard and see right here, you are already on your way. Follow me." Wash pushed herself up from the desk and marched across the room toward a closed door.

Chrys quickly followed. She looked around the big room at the other detectives and their desks trying to get a sense of what was going on. Wash opened a door and stepped aside letting Chrys step up to the threshold. Suddenly the detective's hands were on her. Chrys stumbled forward as she was pushed inside. It was a plain rectangular room with no windows. The walls had giant white boards on them. At this moment they were covered in photographs. One wall had all of the same missing posters as the Hastings window. More even. On the other wall were photographs, most of which she had seen in the

151

flesh. Body parts, limbs, heads and torsos. Some had small photographs of once living faces right beside them. They must have been the parts that were identified. She recognized Joey Love and Darcy Vaughn's pictures next to the limbs found at Leigh Park and in Spencer's truck. This was the murder room. Her eyes took in everything.

"All of these people, all of these men and women are dead," Wash' voice was sharp. "Yes, I know about all of the missing. This arm here," her finger stabbed at a photograph of an arm which was decayed enough to show the bone beneath flesh, "Could have been this Bobbi." She crossed to the missing wall and stabbed a picture of a young girl with blond hair and daisy earrings. "Krista here could have been this torso we found half eaten by God knows what. This leg belongs to Heather. This one, Nadia. Ashley, Amy, Rebecca, Lynda, Meghan … all of these young women could be pieces of this disgusting jigsaw puzzle. Then there's the men. Do you know what's different from the men and women? The men had more pieces cut out of them. Flesh cut off of them like steaks from a kill. You know about that, don't you? People eating human flesh? And do you want to know something else, little girl? The medical examiner says most of these limbs and flesh were cut off while the victims were alive." Wash yanked Chrys back to the main room by her shoulder and slammed the door. The detective's face was burning with anger. "We don't know how he took them. We don't know where he took them or what happened to them. All we know is where they ended up. We have over thirty-two victims to investigate from this one spot. I don't have the time for this childish Nancy Drew act. Go back to your restaurant and stay there."

There was silence. Even the others in the room seemed to be waiting for one of them to say or do something. They didn't wait long. Chrys said, "Was Crystal Stone one of the identified victims?"

Wash sighed. She was so tired. "Get out of my police station."

~ * ~

Her second stop was Hastings. It was different by daylight. It seemed dirtier. At night it was still gritty, but there was more to look at and so many people you couldn't see the filth. During the day it was almost empty of people. The homeless took over where the hookers and dealers ruled the night. Stores were open and there were people, however they wanted in and out as fast as they could. Garbage collected in all the nooks and crannies.

The window of the missing was still there. It had grown in size and thickness. Flowers, stuffed bears, candles that had gone out and mementoes had been placed at the base. Chrys wondered if it was in a better neighborhood would there be a TV news van parked on the street.

She took pictures of the top missing signs before moving some aside and taking more. She found Crystal's missing poster and took two pictures. One was of the entire page and the second a close-up of her necklace. She snapped more pictures of more lost faces. What happened in their lives to bring them here?

Somebody had to know something. Start with the homeless guy sitting by the wall or the tourist couple that looks lost?

After twenty minutes of going up to strangers with the pictures on her phone and asking, "Do you know Crystal," she was feeling hopeless and dirty. She was told to fuck off three times, to go fuck herself twice, propositioned four times and one man exposed himself and told her to suck it. Most people, however, ignored her and walked on.

As per usual, she ignored the texts she got from Jessie.

The missing poster said Crystal disappeared at night. Perhaps this wasn't the right crowd to be asking. It also said she was seen with a man near a mini-van. That wasn't much to go on. Chrys didn't even know what she was going to do with information about the missing woman if she got any. It wasn't going to explain why Hanni had the same necklace. At least she was doing something though.

After walking two blocks in both directions, on both sides of the street, she got back to the yellow beetle and leaned against the passenger door. She didn't know what else she could do. Jessie was texting to ask when she was coming back. There was one text from the dance studio reminding everyone about the Spring Extravaganza costume fitting next week. Sloane sent her a selfie with the tattoo she was working on. A couple of friend's texted random stuff. One texted, "I'm a leaf on the wind," and another said, "Stay shiny." Chrys texted back, "Stay gold."

As she was looking at her phone a text came through from Mr. O'Donnell. He wanted to make sure she was okay. She got a little nervous thinking of the suspected killer being worried about her. When did her brother talk to him and get the moles name? Does that mean the mob boss is mad at them? How dare Spencer put his nose in her business.

Chrys spun around. The hair on the back of her neck tingled. It was that, "Someone's watching me," feeling. Nobody looked out of place. Was that how this killer claimed so many victims? He fit in. He was part of the community. Or he blended.

"Hey."

Chrys held her breath.

"You got a smoke?" A girl stood beside her. She must have been in her late teens. She had short black hair with bright red dyed locks falling down over her forehead. She wore a hooded sweat shirt, the hood only halfway over her head, under a dirty denim jacket, green cargo pants and what looked like army boots that had long lost their shine.

Chrys breathed out, said, "No," and started around the car.

"Do you know what happened to Crystal? You've been asking about her, right?"

Chrys returned back to the sidewalk. "You knew her?"

The girl put her hands in her pockets and pushed the jacket around her. She had braces on her teeth. "Knew her? Like, is she dead?"

"No. I don't know. Do you know her?"

"Do you have a smoke?"

"No," Chrys said. "I can get you a pack I guess. How old are you?"

"Does it matter?"

Is this what Spencer felt like when she had an attitude? "Can I get your name?"

"Feather."

"Feather?"

"Yeah. What of it?"

155

"And how do you know Crystal?" Chrys didn't know if this was going to garner any results, but it was better than nothing.

The girl looked around. "We hung out. I was the last one who saw her, you know." Chrys encouraged her to go on. "We was over by the diner and she went to talk to a guy. The guy talked to her, blew her a kiss all fancy like and she went with him. I ain't seen her since."

"What did the guy look like? How old was he?"

Feather looked up and down the street. A pewter feather earring on one ear dangled back and forth. "I don't know. I don't really remember. He was white. He was a little taller than Crystal." On the missing poster Crystal was listed as being 5'6". "He was, like, average looking. Twenties, thirties, I don't know."

So helpful. "Did you see what car he was driving?"

"A mini-van. Dark. You'd be surprised how many guys come down here in mini-vans. Family men looking for something not so wholesome."

"Did it have any rust? Did you see the license plate?"

"I didn't notice. Are you getting those cigs?"

Chrys' fingers cut through her hair. She was tempted to pull it out. "So there was fuck-all unique about this guy? That's what you're saying."

Feather stepped back. "Don't fucking yell at me, bitch. I don't need to talk to you at all. If I didn't want cigs I wouldn't even have bothered."

"Wait, had you seen him before?"

"I don't know. Maybe. I can't be sure."

"Have you seen him since?"

"Like I said, I don't know. I've been looking around for her, not him. She's my friend, eh." Feather's eyes began to water. She quickly wiped at them. There were yellow stains on her first two fingers.

Chrys could have pushed some more, however she knew it wouldn't accomplish anything. She was looking for an average guy who drove an average mini-van. No problem. "Let's go to the store and get your smokes."

Chrys' brown eyes were wide now. Every man on the street was this psycho. White. She counted fourteen just in the one direction. Average looking. The Mohawk and face tattoo guy was out. Twenties or thirties. Teenagers and old guys were out. She left in the ones wearing hats and glasses. More than half the men she could see in one direction could have been the Wind-Chime Killer. Even her brother fit the description. He was good-looking, but still an average guy. Wylie at the restaurant was probably too tall to be considered average. Ranger, yes. Gordie, no. Mr. O, definitely. Anyone could be the killer. There had to be something unique about this guy. Nobody could go through life without leaving some sort of mark on the world.

As she handed the cigarette package to Feather she said, "Did you say something about the guy blowing Crystal a kiss?"

"Yeah." Feather had the pack open in seconds flat. The plastic wrap fell to the sidewalk.

"What do you mean by that?" Chrys took a second to pick up the wrap and shoved it in her pocket.

"Like this." Feather plucked the already lit cigarette from her mouth, laid her hand flat in front of her mouth and blew smoke across her palm and over her fingers toward Chrys.

Chapter 23

"Server! I need a server." Spencer didn't care how loud he was. He slid the finished plates under the heat-lamp and gave the butcher's-block table a quick wipe down.

"Spence, we need to talk." Chrys was in the black server's uniform. She had been trying to talk to her brother since she got home and spent a little time on his computer, but he was either ignoring her or trying to distract her.

"I need you to deliver these to table fourteen."

She looked down at the two plates. One was a NY strip steak with baby potatoes, vegetables and a pepper sauce. The other was fettucine Alfredo. They just reminded her she hadn't eaten today. "That's not my section."

"Come on, Chrys. We're under staffed and for some reason busy as fuck. And I'm barely holding on. Just deliver the food."

"Have you talked to Hanni?"

"Food. Table fourteen. Go." He spun on the ball of his foot and put his attention back on the sauté pans. His sister grumbled something, but with the exhaust fan and restaurant noises he couldn't hear. He didn't bother looking to see if she took the plates. He knew she would.

Spencer looked at the order chits. "Fire second course for table twenty. Two fish and chips."

"Two fish and chips," Ranger said with a nervous shake to his voice.

"You gots dis Ranger!" Gordie bellowed.

Spencer had second guessed having the fish and chips for dinner on a Friday night. The full responsibility fell on the young fry-cooks shoulders. The decision was made to take some of the pressure off of the chef and sous chef. Spencer was thinking a drink would be good right about now.

"Cold apps ready for table three." Mallory had two Alcrest salads, a scallop ceviche and a plate of oysters ready on the side of her table.

Spencer spun to face the pass. "Server! I need a server."

"I got it. New order for you."

"Thanks, Sue. New order. Table six. Four covers. Two Alcrest salads, one mussels. Second course, peppercorn strip medium, fish and chips, penne Bolognese, chicken."

All three of the other cooks repeated their parts of the order.

"Mal, give me six minutes on the salads."

"Six minutes, heard."

It took nearly fifteen minutes before Chrys was back at the pass. "Have you talked to Hanni yourself?"

Spencer looked up from the chits he was organizing. "Two hours ago. She's still shook up from finding all those body parts. Let it be."

"But I think I know how he gets his victims." Her hand went down on the pass. The finger brace made a different noise than her usual thumb ring.

"Chrys, watch your voice." Spencer took a quick drink. This time it was ice water in a yogurt container. "How many times do you have to be told to stay out of it?"

"Chef, may I?" Wylie called from behind the cold-side table.

Spencer looked at his sister a moment longer hoping to get his point across before putting his attention on Wylie. "Go ahead."

"How long for the bar meals?"

"Shit!" Behind him was a collection of pans all with cooked food at different stages. His mind did a quick calculation. "Give me three minutes."

"Okay, they're getting impatient."

"Two minutes." Spencer called out. He had forgot about the order for the two people sitting at the bar. "Are you guys ready? Three tables at once. I'm getting these two bar plates out first. Ranger, I need a plate with rice and veg." He handed over a plate from the oven they used as a warmer. "Follow those with steak frites rare, poached halibut, fish and chips, Alcrest salad and pepper steak mid-rare."

Behind him Chrys growled her disappointment and stomped off. She waited until there was a lull in service before returning to the pass for anything other than food. "You remember I told you about Crystal who had the same necklace as the one given to Hanni?" Her brother was leaning on the butcher's-block. Sweat ran down his temple. "The last time she was seen someone blew her a kiss like this." She showed him the way Feather showed her.

161

"So what?"

"I Googled "blow a kiss drug" and it came up with scopolamine or Devil's Breath."

"Hold on. Gordie, you have the kitchen. I'll be in the back if you need me." Spencer signaled his sister to follow him to the back.

She continued as they walked. "This drug, it makes you do whatever you're told like an obedient slave. People have emptied their bank accounts, helped thieves load up their own belongings, been raped and who knows what else because the victims can't remember anything. One guy brought people up to his place and helped these guys bring his stuff downstairs and into a truck. The doorman didn't notice anything wrong with him. Colombian criminals have used it to steal peoples stuff. It's odorless and tasteless. People come to three days later and know nothing."

"So what is this guy making his victims do?" Spencer dropped into his chair behind his desk.

"I don't know. Josef Mengele, the Nazi Angel of Death, used it as a truth serum. Wash said the victims were alive when they got cut up. Maybe he uses it so that they let him cut them up. I don't know."

"And where does he get this drug?"

"South America. It comes from a tree down there."

"Did you tell Wash?"

"Fuck that, Spence. She doesn't care what I have to say. She'd probably put me in jail." Chrys leaned with her shoulder and side of her head touching the upright freezer. Her brother was listening to her and that was good.

"Chrys, I think you're getting obsessed. You're looking for things that aren't there. Leave this stuff to the cops."

162

"What the fuck, Spence? I'm not kidding about this. This is all real."

"I'm sure it is, but you're finding connections because you want to. Hanni gets a necklace that happens to be similar to the one this missing girl had. Then a guy blew her a kiss, so of course there is a drug for it. I bet you can Google random shit like a turtle-pig and find things on it. You have to stop this."

"Spencer," Jessie leaned through the doorway, "They need you out front."

"Be right there." He waited until he was certain Jessie was gone. "Let Detective Washburn do her job. And Hanni is fine."

"She got a present from a psycho." Chrys was talking with her hands. "How is that fine?"

Spencer got up from the chair. "She got a present from a customer she flirted with. It's not the first time."

"Is she really that good of a lay, brother dear?"

"That's enough, Chrys." Spencer walked passed her and out of the office without another word. He bit down on his tongue to keep himself from saying anything he'd regret later. Tomorrow after the Farmers' Market he would go by Hanni's and actually see that she was okay. That didn't mean he was believing his sister.

Chrys pounded her fist against the freezer. She felt a twinge in her wrist. She was willing to bet that she was right. Tomorrow she'd start finding out who this guy was. She just had to figure out how to do that.

Chapter 24

Everyone forgets things. "Oh crap. I left the door unlocked all night. Good thing I'm in a safe neighborhood." Hilarious. All you need to open a locked door is a minute amount of knowledge on how to pick locks. Practice makes you better, however if the person in the house forgets to lock the back door where they parked their car then it's easy to just walk in.

Not to mention how many people don't lock the door leading from the garage to the house.

I can hear the water running.

I walk through the kitchen. There are a few dirty dishes in the sink. She had soup and wine. She doesn't eat much. I know this because I've been watching her.

They took away my play place, so now I have to have fun in other ways. What am I going to do with this one? It was the others fault that Grandpa's place is gone to me. How can I make them all pay?

The sound of running water is coming from down the hallway. I slip my hand in my pocket and take a fist full of the powder that is all mine. I can take her now.

There's steam coming out of the open bathroom door. She's all alone in her house. As far as she knows the outside door is locked so why on earth should she shut the bathroom door, let alone lock it? She's in the shower. It seems kind of late for her to be going out. I know she's not scheduled for work at the restaurant.

I left my shoes at the door, so my feet are very quiet.

She has music playing from a small stereo beside the sink that her towel hangs over. Her clothes are on the floor. Shorts, a T-shirt, lace panties. From the bathroom doorway I can see the outline of her through the misted glass. Her hands soap up her body. I could kill her right now. End it all and devastate the others. I'm getting hard just thinking about her screams, their screams.

I return to the main room. I could take her, have her cut her own arm off.

Bing.

She left her cell phone on the counter. The name on the front is that of the lion. Damn him. He shouldn't miss out on all the fun.

Chapter 25

"Last night was crazy," Jessie said. "It hasn't been like that in a while."

"We survived though and nobody got yelled at." Spencer dropped a box of knives on the table next to the "Old Goat's Knife Sharpener" sign. "I wish we could have more nights like that. Hey, Pete, can I get all of these sharpened please?"

The white haired man peaked into the box. He was an old goat. "Give me thirty minutes."

"We'll be back." Spencer turned to Jessie. "Do you want a sausage on a bun?"

"No thanks. I'm saving myself for the mini-doughnuts."

The Farmers' Market was in a large building with green and white walls and a red tin roof. There were a few booths outside such as the knife sharpener and the barbeque selling locally made sausages. On the front steps a man was making balloon animals. Sometimes there was live music. The main focus of the market was for everyday people to buy from local farmers without them having to leave the city. British Columbia had a longer growing season than the rest of the country, which made it possible to get vegetables that were not in season anywhere else. It was a great thing for farm-to-table restaurants. The Farmers' Market also housed artists, a traditional cheese maker, baking, naturally made clothing, a smoothie booth and food from different countries like Ukraine, Morocco and China. On one end was a butcher's booth. The far end had a place that sold seasoned oils and there was the mini-doughnut booth, of course. From what they heard there was a long waiting list to get a booth.

They were early and people were already walking around with little brown paper bags overflowing with the tasty doughnuts and bags full of things they had purchased. For some going to the market was work related. For others it was a family tradition. Closer to lunch time it would fill up with tourists.

Spencer and Jessie maneuvered around and through the people going in and out of the front entrance. He bit his tongue when they had to step around people who stopped to chat. At least there were no baby strollers. Too late. He gave an awkward smile to the mother who had stopped to inquire about perogies and cabbage rolls. Her monstrosity of a stroller probably cost more than a small apartment in the downtown and she was sure to leave it sticking out into the aisle.

Jessie tugged on his arm. She had to go up on her toes to speak in his ear. "I'm going to go get my doughnuts. You do what you do and we'll meet up."

"Okay. I'll be on the other side."

The building was a long rectangle with booths all around the inside walls and down the middle creating a loop. Spencer nodded at the woman running the butcher's booth

168

that sold sausages, jerky and an assortment of meat cuts from all different types of animals. It was the same butcher that was on his street and he used at the restaurant – the one he owed money to. It was the Mrs. that always brought it up. Spencer put his head down and walked on.

"Stop right there, Spencer Alcrest."

Crap. He stopped and stepped to the side. He still wouldn't look the woman in the eye. "I know I have to bring you guy's money. I promise I will next week."

"What for? You're paid off. I wanted to tell you we have the buffalo you like." Her short black hair was painted with silver.

Spencer looked her in the eye. "What do you mean I'm paid off?"

"Chrys came to the shop last week and paid everything. Do you want to look at the buffalo?"

"I'll come back after." He took a step back into the flow. "Excuse me," he had to step around a man looking at a display of handmade rings. Chrys paid off his bill at the butcher's … what the hell was that?

It was the vegetables on the other side that he was looking for. Spencer wasn't sure what he wanted, but vegetables were something he could afford. Of course, since his sister paid his bill perhaps he could afford more. One step at a time. The vegetable gardener he liked was around the corner between a homemade jeweler booth and the hippies that took the hair and fur off their farm animals and made clothing from them. It always looked like itchy stuff.

Spencer let out a sigh the moment he stepped out of the continuously moving wave of people that circled the market. He smiled at the lady behind the vegetable table before looking down. There was fresh lettuce, a few baskets of new potatoes, bunches of beets, carrots, string beans, peppers … it was a mountain of colours and freshness. He couldn't really go wrong.

"Hey."

Spencer looked at the man who spoke beside him, but didn't recognize him. "Hi." He got that feeling like he should know this man, however couldn't place him. The best he could say was that he was average looking. Just some guy.

"I should eat more vegetables," the man said.

Spencer nodded. He needed something different for tonight's veg. If they were lucky they'd be as busy as last night. He held up a bunch of beets by the stems. The leaves, dark green with purple veins draped over his hand. He could use those as an actual green sautéed with bacon and garlic. The beet bulbs were dark purple and dangled beneath his fist. They'd lighten slightly in the cooking process and would get an amazing shine. He could use the water he was going to boil them in, plus a few of the beets for borscht soup. The rest would make a unique vegetable.

"I never know what to do with beets," the man beside him stated. "Grandma would pickle them."

"You can do lots with them. They make a great side vegetable." Spencer put the beets down and indicated to the lady watching them closely that he wanted a box full of them.

The man held some up in the air close to his face. "Don't they bleed?"

Spencer didn't even realize that was a question. He didn't want to be answering cooking inquires all day and not this early. Today was not the day he was going to enjoy teaching. He just wanted to get back to the restaurant and get on with the day.

He looked at the man. The beets were up close to his face. He gently swung them side to side so that they bounced off each other.

Spencer paid cash for his box. "When you cook them, yeah, they can bleed. Price you have to pay. I'm cooking these at The Alcrest Gastropub tonight and this weekend if you want to come try them."

"I'll do that. They're like silent wind-chimes." The man's voice dropped to a whisper. "How lovely." He put the beets down.

Spencer stared at the vegetables then looked up at the man. "What did you say?" Did he really hear that? Who would refer to beets as a silent wind-chime? He took the box of beets that was handed to him.

As the man said, "Well, I have to go see about honey," he turned away.

"What?" Spencer had to adjust his hands around the box. He took a step. Someone bumped his arm. He planted himself and balanced to keep the box from falling. As he looked up the man was gone. Spencer thought he saw his head in the crowd flowing away, but that could have been anyone. What did he say? Honey. Wind-chimes. Why would he say those things? The beets were like silent wind-chimes. Like, like the limbs hanging from a tree?

Hanni.

Spencer pushed into the crowd using the box of beets as a plow. He ignored people telling him to watch out and slow down as he pushed through them. The mini-doughnut place was just around the corner. Jessie was already dipping into her brown paper bag.

"Do you want one?"

"He was here. Did you see him?" Spencer looked around with wide eyes. "The killer. The killer was here. We have to go. Chrys was right." He said, "Come on, this way," as he headed for a fire exit.

"Spencer, slow down."

The bright daylight blinded Spencer for a moment as they burst through the door. His eyes scanned the back parking lot. If that guy wanted a quick out he would have come this way. Where was he?

"What did he look like?" All Jessie could see was people coming and going from the Farmers' Market. Nobody looked out of place or like a Criminal Minds bad guy. The only people she saw walking away was a family of four heading to their car and a woman carrying plastic bags. She didn't know who they were looking for.

"He was like," Spencer couldn't really place how tall the man was. "He had," was it brown or black hair? Was he wearing a hat? Maybe he was blond. Forget about what he was wearing. Spencer never noticed. "He said something about wind-chimes and then checking on Hanni. I could be jumping to conclusions but I don't think he was talking about bee hives."

"What do you want to do?"

Spencer took another look around letting his gaze scan all of the cars. "Let's go see Hanni." If Chrys is right this guy was going to do far worse things to Hanni than what happened to Spencer before. This psycho was going to make her do what he wanted and that hadn't turned out well for anyone else.

"What about the knives?"

"I can get them later. Jess, I know this is, whatever it is, but I have to go check on her."

"Its fine, Spencer. Let's go." Jessie took the lead. "Do you really think this guy is after Hanni?" Both of their breaths came fast as they jogged around the building.

"Chrys thinks so. You didn't see what he did to those people. I can't let another one get hurt."

Chapter 26

They say, what you don't know can't hurt you. What I know can.

Spencer. Spencer the lion. He doesn't know I'm here. He doesn't know I was sitting in my van on the street watching his den. He doesn't know I saw him get in the bright yellow bug after the driver honked, a most excellent vehicle to follow, and doesn't know I'm following him and the one with the short brown hair into the Farmers' Market.

He hasn't texted Hanni since last night when I answered him. Her phone is in my pocket. I'd feel it vibrate if he did. He has no idea where she is. He thinks she's safe and sound at home recovering from the shock of finding my chimes. That only took her a day. He doesn't know. He's no predator.

I watch him drop off a box at the knife sharpeners before going to the front doors. He could look behind him and all he'd see is a crowd of faces.

This isn't how I normally do things. I go for that one person. I go for the individual scream and fear. I pluck the ones nobody would really notice are missing. A missing poster is as far as it goes. I wanted something different, and now I have it. This is terrorism. Creating fear. Letting it rise to a boil until you can't control the reaction.

I almost walk into him. A woman with a baby stroller is in his way and I stop myself before walking into him.

Spencer's friend goes off toward the end and he strolls around. He's avoiding people. He gets caught by someone and I walk past. A display of rings will occupy my time as I watch him over my shoulder.

"Excuse me."

I don't say anything, but then follow him to the next booth. I don't hear him take a breath, but I feel it.

"Hey," I say as a greeting. His gaze falls on me quickly as he returns the greeting. I'm not a friend, colleague or fellow chef. I'm nobody to him and don't warrant any more than, "hi."

I didn't come here to be nothing. "I should eat more vegetables."

He nods, but the chef wants to ignore me. The lion doesn't know he's being hunted.

He picks up a bunch of beets. The purple beetroot swings beneath their leaves and bounce against each other just like one of those metal ball things on businessmen's desks. They remind me of something else.

I tell him about how Grandma would pickle them. I leave out that the jars were kept in the storm cellar where Grandpa would butcher the friends he made. I wish I had known him. Mother has told me stories. She would sneak down there and watch what he was doing. She remembers their screams. She told me about how the blood soaked into the clay floor, darkening it. A family tradition if you will. It was not long after that I was born.

176

"Don't they bleed?" I blink and look at the lion. Did he hear me? Did the words actually leave my mouth? I pick up the same bunch of beets and swing them side to side.

He's actually inviting me to his restaurant. It's like having an open door into his den.

I stare at the beets in my hand. I remember Grandpa's wind-chimes always making noise. Always kept greeting me when I went there. There was always that hollow sound of metal and wood all around the house. I swing the beets again. "They're like silent wind-chimes. How lovely."

"What did you say?"

I drop the beets. I didn't mean to say anything. He's looking at me strange. He can see through the shadow.

"Well," I step back into the river of people, "I have to go see about Hanni."

I turn and quickly go with the flow of people. As a shadow I twist and turn through the crowd, never looking back. As a predator I'm on the run. I let my true self be seen. I have to move. I have to be quick. He may have seen who I am and now it's time to go.

It's too soon though.

I go through a side exit into the sunlight. The side parking lot is out in front of me. It's already full. People are heading for the market as a few go for their vehicles. A woman alone.

Did I show my hand?

I want things to last with her. I want to feel her scream. I want to bathe in it. The lion can't have her.

The new prey is going near my van. There is no such thing as coincidence. This is meant to be. She has bags in her hands. She probably wants to drop these off before returning inside. She won't be able to stop my attack. Silly woman for wandering away from the herd.

With a glance over my shoulder I see the lion and his friend looking, but they can't see me. My van will hide us from everyone.

This isn't my usual way. I'm taking too much of a risk. My hand goes in the bag in my pocket. I can't stop myself. She's not my preferred choice. She'll be missed. Alarms will be rung. She won't be just forgotten like all of the others. I need this. I need the chase. I need the fear of the people.

"Excuse me, ma'am."

She looks at me. I blow the white powder in her face as I walk by. She stumbles back and drops her bags to the ground. Potatoes roll out onto the flattened grass. She wipes at her face with both hands, but can't stop what's happening. Tears flow down her face.

And then it takes and she stands still. Her eyes glaze over. Her arms go down at her sides. She's mine.

Chapter 27

Elaine Vogt couldn't believe her luck. Where else in the country could you get beets, new potatoes, baby carrots and squash all at the same time of year? The plan was to pickle the beets and carrots. Dwayne was itching to barbeque tonight and the baby potatoes would be great with butter and garlic powder all wrapped in tinfoil. He was at the butcher's booth on the far end of the market at that very moment seeing what meat he could find. Perhaps Elaine would try doing a quick pickle of the carrots for tonight's supper. She saw it on a cooking show last weekend and wanted to try it. Either way it was going to be a nice start to the barbeque season.

"I'm going to take these out to the car," she said to her husband as he knelt down to look in the glass display at the butcher's booth.

All he answered with was, "uh-huh."

"Mommy, can I come?" Their daughter had insisted on wearing her sparkly gymnastic leotard this morning.

"No, you stay with Daddy."

179

"But, what about the donuts? You said." That was just how she said it, donuts.

Elaine was already being swept along with the crowd as she replied with, "We will Baby. I'll be right back."

As she tried distributing the bags into one hand Elaine thought about the mess her daughter was going to make. She'd probably want the chocolate sauce on the doughnuts too. Elaine could imagine the chocolate drips and crumbs on her leotard and the back seat of the car.

Her hand was in her pocket getting the keys when she heard a voice. Elaine turned.

Something hit her face. Shock made her breathe in as she stepped back away from it. Something burned her nostrils. Her back hit a mini-van. The bags fell from her fingers. Her hands flew up to her face trying to wash it away.

The drug already coursed through her veins. There was no fighting it. She felt whatever it was flashing lightning against her brain. It attacked her nervous system destroying any self-thought. There were colours and lights and images she didn't recognize. She was no longer Elaine Vogt.

A voice instructed her to get in the van.

Chapter 28

"Chrysanthemum, you're out early." Liam O'Donnell looked like he had been up for a while. He wore khaki pants and a tan silky shirt. His hair was perfect.

Chrys heard her brother's alarm in the morning for him to go to the Farmers' Market and instantly opened her eyes. She was dressed and had her hair tied back before he probably had coffee in his travel mug. She waited until she heard the door shut then called a cab to come get her.

"Sorry to bother you at home." Chrys didn't expect O'Donnell to answer the door himself. She expected a maid, an English butler named Geoffrey or at least one of his guards, but not the man himself. She thought she'd still have a few minutes to think about what to say. "I, I wanted to apologize for Spence."

He stepped aside. "Come in. I was just brewing a pot of coffee."

She could smell the wonderful aroma as she stepped inside. The house was very modern. Her ankle boots clicked on the hardwood floor. The sitting furniture was white. The rest of it was black or natural wood. There were gorgeous paintings on the walls, small sculptures on stands (all of which looked expensive) and flowers near every window. Not a dust speck to be seen. O'Donnell led the way into a large kitchen with all stainless steel appliances and marble countertops. Spencer would have loved it. Chrys wondered if much cooking happened here.

He motioned for her to sit on a stool at a breakfast nook as he went around it and started with the motions of getting cups and pouring coffee.

"I wasn't going to ask for your source in the police station. I needed it to find out what I needed." Chrys drew designs on the marble with a fingertip. "I was going to take the punishment." The finger brace clicked. She tapped her thumb ring on the countertop. It sounded different than the pass at the restaurant.

"What did Spencer tell you about our conversation? Sugar?"

She squeezed her lips together. "Do you have hot chocolate mix?"

"No."

"Then yeah, lots of sugar. Spence didn't say anything to me. Detective Washburn told me." Chrys wasn't sure how she should feel. At the office down at the docks she was perfectly calm. She dealt with numbers, answered phones and spoke to whoever came in. She handed the suspected mobster paperwork and went on with life. Here she was in his private home and she was nervous. At work there were video cameras everywhere. She had yet to see one. Her eyes searched every corner without seeing any, but she was sure they were there. There weren't even guards. She was nervous to be alone with the man. "Did you two talk about something I should know?"

"Chrysanthemum, there's always more to a story. However, this one is between Spencer and myself. None of it was your fault."

None of what? "So I still have a job?" Her voice was playful. She could fake it. She knew the stories and had heard O'Donnell yell at people – still it didn't scare her. She was certain there were things Spencer kept to himself about their relationship. And she knew nothing of the relationship between Rene Alcrest and Liam O'Donnell.

"Oh my God!" Chrys had taken a sip of the coffee he had slid across to her. He also placed a bowl of sugar on the countertop. "This is like, the best cup of coffee I've ever had."

"Ethiopian. Rated best in the world."

"It's good."

"And to answer your question, yes, you still have your job. Now tell me about the eye, wrist and finger."

"Defending a clown and fighting a wolf." She told him about trying to find the killer and that everyone had it wrong. "I know this is a lot, but do you have anyone else in the police station? I'm stuck. I don't know what else to do."

O'Donnell shook his head. "I don't have anyone else that can help you. I don't think the detectives have much that would help anyway." He took a drink of his coffee and licked his lips. "My advice would be to follow what you know. You can't follow what you don't. I'd also suggest staying out of it, but I know you better than you think."

Chrys gave him a smile as her eyes dropped. She didn't feel good about what he just said. How well did he know her? "I should probably go. I'll call a cab."

"Glenn is coming to give my friend a ride. I'm sure he can drop you off. Finish your coffee. Can't let something that good go to waste."

She left her phone in her bra and sipped more of the sugary, yet bitter in a good way, Ethiopian blend. Friend, what did O'Donnell mean by friend? She had yet to hear anyone moving around. There was not even anything around that would say someone else was in the building. Was it a woman? A man? He knew a lot of famous people, so there was no telling who it could be. Chrys fought the urge to twist around in her chair and look for clues.

After a moment of silence O'Donnell said, "You haven't taken me up on my offer to tell you about your mother."

He had given her the offer over a year ago and brought it up almost every time they met. Chrys had wondered when he would bring it up to her at work, but he was always professional. "I don't know if I want to. No offence, but the fact that you know something about her isn't very encouraging."

He had a friendly laugh. "I knew yer father more."

She held her breath. Chrys remembered very little about her mother. She worked a lot. Every morning Chrys would be dropped off at a daycare and her mom would pick her up at 5:00pm. They would go to their apartment and play games and dress-up until bedtime. Until that day that she didn't show up and at 6:00pm a social workers van pulled up out front of the daycare. Chrys screamed and fought but her mom never came back.

She didn't remember a father. She never knew him. She had asked the Alcrest's questions but they knew nothing. They were only foster parents who took her in. They only knew what they were told from her file. She had

184

a couple pictures of her mom, so she knew she was pretty. Always smiling. There were none of a man. Chrys had never really thought about it.

"You knew my father?"

"Ay. He was a friend once." O'Donnell took his cup to the sink.

"Once?" Her voice was sharp as a blade. "Is he dead? Did you kill him?"

The Irishman leaned back against the counter. His eyes stared at her. They were soft and caring. Chrys hated that he looked like just an average guy. "He is dead, and no, I didn't kill him. Do you want to know who he was?"

Chrys turned at the noise of stiletto heels on the hardwood.

The woman was almost six feet in her six inch heels. Straight blond hair fell down over her shoulders. Green eyes stared at the Aboriginal woman with instant recognition. Hanni wore tight faded jeans and a turquoise blouse with her navel and cleavage both showing. Her make-up was impeccable and looked more like she was going out to a party than going home after … after what? She had the strap to a large bag in her hand, it almost dragged on the floor. She stopped walking and stared at Chrys. Liam O'Donnell's lips were in a satisfied smirk. Hanni took a breath before continuing forward.

"Liam, I'm ready."

"WHAT THE FUCK?" Chrys' jaw dropped.

O'Donnell ignored the outburst. He crossed the room to Hanni passing her an envelope and pressing his lips on her cheek. Her hand went to his face and turned it so that she could press her lips to his. "Glenn is outside waiting. I told Chrysanthemum she could get a ride too. You don't mind sharing, do you?" As he turned back to Chrys his fingers wiped lipstick from his own lips.

Hanni's eyes fired lasers at Chrys who was wide-eyed and mouthing obscenities. "Not a problem," Hanni said with her wicked smile. She sniffed. "Same time next week?"

"I may be busy. I've passed your name onto some colleagues, so you might be busy yourself." O'Donnell led her to the front door. "Go wait in the car. I need to finish telling Chrysanthemum something."

"What the fuck," Chrys repeated when she climbed into the back of the town-car ten minutes later. She had a lot to process and the first was the surprise appearance of the bitch.

The car started down the street.

Hanni sat on the far side staring out the window. "I'm sure you've figured it out." Her words were cold. "What happened to your face?

"We're not talking about me." Chrys turned her entire body to face her. "You're a hooker."

"Escort!"

What the fuck? "There's a difference? I knew you were a slut but I didn't think you were a professional one."

"There's a big difference," Hanni turned to look at her. "I'm a companion. I don't sleep with anyone unless I want to. For most of my clients, even Liam its dinner and conversation or they take me on business retreats or events. When we are out late e lets me sleep over. I'm arm candy."

"And you screw them."

"If I want to. That's my dicision."

"And you get paid for it."

"I get paid for my time, yes. Just like you do when you teach a dance class."

"Do you get paid more for fucking?" Chrys' mouth was dry. She didn't get what was going on.

"I'm not talking about this with you."

"Did you screw Liam?"

"That's none of your business."

If ever there needed a definition for the phrase "mind blown" someone could have taken a picture of Chrys' face at that moment. "How much does he pay you?"

"A thousand dollars a night."

Chrys' finger flew out at her. "You're entertainment! On his balance sheets there's always a write-off of a thousand dollars under entertainment and that's you. Holy shit."

"Chrys, you can't tell anyone."

"Oh sure. If you can shit out balloon animals I won't tell anyone. I'm telling Spencer."

"Chrys, you can't."

Chrys shook her hair out. "Is this like, for your drugs or something? Are you putting yourself through med school?"

Hanni watched the buildings go by. It didn't take long to know you had left the rich, high end part of Middleton. She didn't like having to return to the middle class. "I don't have a drug problem and I'm not really doing anything else. I like money, Chrys. I like buying things. I like going places. I don't think there's anything wrong with that. There've been some weeks where I've made over five grand."

"Five thousand? In a week?" It was Chrys' turn to look out her window.

"And my clients are nice to me."

187

Chrys looked back at her. She didn't really know this woman. "How long have you been doing this? How have you kept it a secret?" Her thoughts were all over the place. $5000 per week for doing what (if Chrys was being honest with herself) she herself really enjoyed doing, did not sound that bad. Two months and she could have her own place and car.

Hanni's teeth glistened as she smiled. "I've been doing it for a while. I have a web site and a fake name. Plus my clients don't run in the same circles as people I know. If we go out for dinner and dancing it's just a date. I've been to gallery openings and the theatre. I've been flown to Hollywood parties. My website doesn't show my face and has a private phone number that nobody knows. I'm not hurting anyone."

"What about Spence?" Chrys' cell phone binged so she pulled it out to see who texted her. "Speak of the devil."

"Miss Holden, you're home. Miss Alcrest, am I taking you to the Alcrest?" Glenn's sapphire eyes looked at them through the rearview mirror. The amount of information that guy must know.

Chrys looked up from her phone. "I'll stay here."

"What for? I don't want you here."

As soon as they were out of the car Chrys took Hanni by the arm and pulled her toward the house. "Spencer is on his way here." Their steps quickened. "He hasn't heard from you in days and I have him convinced the psycho killer is after you."

"What the hell?"

"Don't use that tone with me skank. You haven't talked to Spence in days."

"I lost my phone."

"Yeah, right." Chrys' gaze went up and down the street looking for Jessie's bright yellow bug as Hanni unlocked her door. As soon as it was open she pushed the other inside.

"I'm serious. I was getting ready for my date with Liam," Chrys' snicker made her pause for a second, "and when I got out of the shower and ready I couldn't find my phone. Glenn was already waiting, so I left."

"Well, I think this psycho is actually after you, so there." Chrys peaked out the curtains. "Where's your car?"

"I park in the back. Why would this guy be after me? What did I do?"

Chrys lowered her voice as she took another look out. "He likes hookers."

"What was that?"

Chrys looked at her with doe eyes. "What? I didn't say anything. Why don't you get in your car, go to the Alcrest and call Spencer from there. Make up some story about where you were, therapy, your mom's, something. I'll get him out of here. I'll say I broke in to look around and you weren't here. That alright by you, Miss Holden? Who is Holden anyway?"

"My professional name is Nikki Holden. It's a character from a book."

"You can read?" Chrys glared at Hanni. "Oh, and after all this I want you to stop seeing my brother. Stop seeing him or I tell him."

The two women stared at each other. They were testing each other. The question was how important was one thing or the other. Was seeing Spencer important enough to Hanni that she would risk calling Chrys' bluff and if Chrys

189

was not bluffing would he even stay with her? Or was he a conquest and now that she had him was that enough?

"You're a real bitch, you know that?" Hanni said. "Who did Liam say was your father? Some competing crime boss? A contract killer? A useless bum?"

Chrys stared through the tiniest space between curtain and window frame. Her teeth pressed into her lip. "He didn't say. I told him I didn't want to know." A tear ran down her cheek. She was glad Hanni was behind her and couldn't see. "They're here. Stay in the back room. Wait until I get them out of here then go."

Jessie pulled her yellow Volkswagen up to the curb in front of Hanni's house. There was nothing out of the ordinary. The neighborhood had the look and noises you would expect for a Saturday morning. A man was mowing his lawn. Kids could be heard playing. Someone was walking a dog. Bad things don't happen in nice neighborhoods.

Spencer crossed the yard to Hanni's front door faster than he had the last time he was here. His heart raced. Chances were Hanni was going to answer the door. She had to. He pounded his fist against it and waited. Nothing. As he cupped his hands around his face and got close to the window he thought about what he would do if he saw hanging limbs. A forearm with white-tipped nails on the fingers. Nothing moved inside.

"Maybe she's asleep." Jessie's voice was calming. She tried smoothing out her husky tone. "It's still kind of early for her, isn't it?"

Spencer took out his phone and speed dialed Hanni's number as he banged on the door again. Hanging at the side of the porch was a wind-chime made of hollow metal tubes dangling beneath a pyramid. The sound it made was pretty. He couldn't remember if it was there before.

The front door opened. Spencer stepped back. Jessie moved to avoid him.

The person inside the door wasn't Hanni. She wasn't even blond.

"Chrys!"

"Hanni's not here." Chrys stepped out and shut the door behind her. She bounded down the steps passed the two others.

"What the hell, Chrys?" Spencer didn't know what he was supposed to do. "Chrys!"

"What?" She turned around but didn't stop moving away. She needed them to follow her and not look around the back of the house.

"What? This what." He pointed at the door and her. "What the hell are you doing here? How did you get in?" He jumped down the steps and grabbed his sister's arm. "Where are you going?"

"Nobody believed me about Crystal's necklace or the drug or anything. I had to fucking check." At first Chrys pulled away, then gave in and stood still. "I got a taxi here and picked the lock on the back door." She had worked for the locksmith on the same street as the restaurant long enough to learn some tricks, so it was possible and her brother knew it. "Nothing's gone. Nothing's disturbed. She's just not here."

"Then why are you taking off so quick?"

"Because I don't need a lecture from you about sticking my nose where it doesn't belong and that I'm putting myself in danger. Something is wrong, Spencer." Tears were welling up in Chrys' big eyes. This was no act, only it wasn't about the killer. "Why did you text asking if I had seen her? Why are you here?"

"I know," Spencer stated. "The killer talked to me." He told his sister about his encounter at the Farmers' Market.

"How long have you been here?"

"Half hour. Maybe longer."

"He didn't come here then. He didn't have time."

"Then where is he?" Jessie asked.

Chrys yanked her arm away from her brother and pointed a finger at his face. "I told you. You didn't want to believe me, but I so told you. Now the guy probably has her because nobody wanted to listen. I so fucking told you." Okay, she knew she was going over the top, but she was right and he was wrong. Plus it was working.

"Guys," Jessie put one hand on Spencer and raised another to Chrys. "Maybe we should talk about this somewhere else."

Spencer exhaled. "I need to go get my knives. And I'm calling Wash."

"Oh it's Wash, now is it? Jessie, Hanni, Wash - I guess we know that Chef prefers blonds."

Jessie shook her hair. "My hair's brown."

"Blond highlights. Same shit." Chrys looked up and down the street. This was a regular street with no taxis unless they were called. This was no New York movie where you could raise an arm and whistle for one. She changed her tone. "Can I get a ride with you guys?"

Chapter 29

"Guys, look." Jessie slowed her car down to a crawl behind the line of other vehicles being diverted past the Farmers' Market. Necks strained to see what was going on.

Up ahead police cars had the entry and exits blocked off. Lights flashed.

"They're not letting anyone in and searching cars going out."

Chrys' head popped up between the two front seats. "You don't think he left Hanni's body parts, do you?" She bit on her bottom lip to stop from laughing at the looks she got.

"No," Spencer said. He had wondered the same thing. With that many people around the killer couldn't have left them hanging anywhere without being seen. The Fish Market was different. It was raining and half-assed secluded. And why would they be searching cars?

"Is that Detective Wash?" Chrys pointed to where they were searching cars as she sneered the woman's nickname. A woman all in grey with a blond ponytail was talking to each driver as uniformed officers looked through the vehicle. "Let me out. We have to tell her what we know."

Both Alcrest's piled out of the car. It wasn't until the uniformed officer started telling them to get back in their vehicle that they yelled for Washburn.

"No!" Wash threw a hand up like a traffic cop telling them to stop. Chrys automatically thought of the Frosty the Snowman song. "I can't deal with you two right now. We have something going on here, so your Nancy Drew – Hardy Boy bullshit is going to have to wait." She watched the officers search another car.

"She's missing." Spencer wouldn't move when a uniformed officer stepped close to him. "She's missing, Detective."

"I know she's missing. Why do you think we're here?"

"How did you know she's missing?"

Wash pushed on both temples. "I should have guessed there would be a connection. How do you two know Elaine Vogt?"

"Who the fucking feneuter is that?" Chrys was yelling loud enough to get everyone's attention. "We're talking about Hanni. Who the hell are you talking about?"

The two women stared at each other. The tension seemed to go off of them in waves like squiggly lines on a comic book page.

Spencer spoke up. "Can we talk to you, Detective?"

Wash looked at him and for a moment he thought she was going to give them what they wanted. "No. Go to the police station and fill out a report."

"Did someone go missing from here?"

"Go away. Both of you."

194

"The killer was here." Spencer pushed the officer's hand away as he stared at Wash. When she looked at him he held his ground.

Wash squeezed her lips together. In a different world when she was this frustrated she would have lashed out with words and fists. It's a trait that got her in trouble more often than not when she was younger. She directed one of her men to take over for her before leading the two Alcrest's away from the commotion. "Now, what the hell are you two talking about?"

Spencer stared at the woman unsure of where to start. Her cheeks were red with anger and her eyes took turns piercing at both of them. For a moment Spencer thought how much she looked like Hanni. She could be an older version. If Hanni was going to grow old, that was. Her lifestyle was one thing, but now a psycho might have her. A lump came up in his throat and he had to look away from the detective's green eyes. He couldn't speak.

Chrys couldn't decide if her brother had love-me-eyes for the detective or if he was seeing something that wasn't there. Either way he wasn't talking. "Spencer talked to the guy. He said he was going after Hanni and now she's – she's not in her house." That wasn't a lie. "If you'd both listened to me from the start none of this would be happening." As she spoke her hands nearly hit her brother. She looked at the detective's confused expression. "You know the missing poster of Crystal Stone? Recall the sun necklace she was wearing? Someone left the same exact necklace for Hanni, a server and Spencer's," Chrys wasn't sure what to call her. She settled with making a face. "Today the fucking psycho talked to Spence here at the

195

Farmers' Market and said he was going after Hanni. Now she's not home."

"Excuse me?"

"That's not exactly right," Spencer added.

"Oh whatever, Spence."

"Hold it!" The two siblings looked at Wash. "The killer? The Wind-Chime Killer? You talked to him? You know who he is?"

Spencer licked his lips then wiped them dry with his fingers. "I don't know if it was him. A guy made a comment about beets being like silent wind-chimes. It creeped me out. Then he said he was going to check on Hanni. I can't honestly say if he meant our friend or, you know, bee honey."

"What did he look like?"

"I don't know."

"Are you serious? How tall was he?"

Spencer shook his head. "I don't know."

Wash pinched the bridge of her nose. "You better go over everything." She didn't let go of her nose until Spencer was done talking about his meeting. "What time was this," was all she asked after he was done.

"About an hour after the market opened."

She glanced over where they were searching cars. A third of the vehicles which had been there when the police first arrived had been gone through. "That's about the same time," Wash didn't mean to say that. She made sure no one was close by, so that she wouldn't get in trouble. "Around that same time Elaine Vogt was going to her car to put some vegetables away. Fifteen minutes later her husband went out looking for her. The bags of vegetables were on the ground beside their car but she was gone. Now you're

196

telling me this guy who has some infatuation with you might have been here? I don't know how he could have taken her."

"Have you heard of Dragons Breath, Detective?" Chrys told her what she had found out about scopolamine. "The victims just do what they are told without a second thought and without remembering. Someone else wouldn't even know they were drugged."

"And you're telling me this why?" Wash had better things to do.

"The last time someone saw Crystal Stone some average looking guy blew her a kiss which happens to be a good way to pass the drug. If you did your job you'd know this."

"Chrys!"

"What?" Chrys' face was red with rage as she turned to Spencer. Her brother being all high and mighty wasn't helping. She looked from one to the other, still unsure what her brother yelled her name for.

Wash had her arms folded in front of her, her fingers drummed on her upper arms. She was apparently an expert at standing-bitch-face. "And where does one get this drug?" Yes, she had heard of scopolamine. The drug had been creeping into the mainstream for years but, as far as she knew, there had been no cases of it in Canada. But then one of the special features of the drug was that the people who were given it couldn't remember a thing.

"South America. It's made from a plant. That's not the point though."

"God damn it, the press is here." Three different vans had pulled onto the grass along the side of the street. People were getting out with video cameras and microphones. "Like I need any of this. Thanks for the

197

information. I'll look into all of it. If you have anything else please stop wasting my time and give a statement to an officer. And like I said, stay out of this. The more you dig in the more dangerous and foolish you seem to be getting." A smirk flashed on Wash' lips. "I have another pressing matter at this time."

"You're such a bitch."

Wash had taken a few steps. She spun quickly. Her ponytail flipped to the other shoulder. "Excuse me?" She marched back and got right in Chrys' face. Spencer expected his sister to back away, but she held her spot firm. Wash seemed slightly surprised. "A mother of a little girl has gone missing in broad daylight. You're giving me guesses and Google searches. Excuse me for doing my job."

"So she's more important than thirty-five hookers and drug addicts? I bet the press would love to hear that." Chrys had to admit the detective smelled nice. For a moment she thought she was going to be thrown to the ground and have handcuffs slapped on her. It wouldn't have been the first time. Though the other cuffs she had slapped on her were pink and fuzzy.

Without another word Detective Washburn spun again and marched away. Both women had made their point. She was on her phone before she was half-way back to where they were still searching cars.

Chrys took a breath which made her body shake. She let her shoulders slump.

Spencer looked at her. She looked tired and deflated like she had been holding it all in and finally being heard took it out of her. "Are you done your crusade for the day?"

198

Her eyes stayed on the ground. "Are you done checking out the cop's ass?"

He stopped himself from replying. "Let's go look for Hanni. There are a lot of places she could be. Maybe this guy didn't take her at all. I mean, if he took this other lady he couldn't have taken her, right? Maybe she's just wasted somewhere."

"Do you really believe that?"

Spencer didn't want to answer. He knew exactly how many victims made up the first wind-chime. "I'll see if I can get my knives and we can go." He was quiet for two minutes without moving. Cars slowly went by on the street. The police did their thing. Then out of the blue he said, "I invited him to dinner this weekend."

"He won't come, Spencer. He's not that stupid." Chrys put her hands in her pockets. She headed to where Jessie had pulled over and parked. She didn't know what else she was supposed to do.

"You never know." Spencer's phone binged. He snatched up the phone and swiped his finger to unlock it. "It's the restaurant. Hello? Hanni?"

Chapter 30

Spencer was out of the car before it was put in park behind The Alcrest.

"Hey Chef. Just having a drag before I get started." Gordie crushed his cigarette beneath his shoe. The bucket he was sitting on creaked as he pushed up.

"Is Hanni here?" Spencer didn't stop. Her car was there, so she had to be. His hand was opening the back door already when he was told she was at the bar.

"I did a prep list." Gordie followed close behind. He really didn't want to get yelled at again. The man had been in the industry for six years and had been yelled at by scarier men than Spencer, but this was a job he liked. "We could use your help. We need just about everything." He got annoyed at Chrys and Jessie trying to push past him. "Any idea where the knives went?"

Spencer put his hand up signaling his sous chef to stop. "Give me a few minutes."

Hanni was there. She sat at the far end bar talking to Megan, the morning server. This week Megan's black hair had a splash of metallic green on the left side and was being held up with chopsticks. Hanni looked refreshed and not like she had escaped from a psycho at all. Her hair flowed. Her face had colour to it.

As Spencer got to her he wrapped his arms around her. "Where have you been?"

Hanni sort of pushed him away without being mean about it. She looked at who was behind him. "What's this about?" She didn't take her hand off his chest.

Chrys had to wonder if that was to hold him back in case he tried hugging her again.

Spencer followed her gaze which was on Chrys and Jessie walking in front of the pass toward them. As his eyes connected with Jessie's she suddenly turned around and headed the other way. During their time together Spencer was never one for public displays of affection. For the longest time he denied to his staff that the two of them were even a couple. And here he was hugging someone she couldn't really stand. He would have to agree that this was one of his top five asshole moments. Nowhere near the top though.

Chrys' hand hit the bar top. Pain shot from her finger up her arm. Her face cringed. "What the fuck, bitch? It's been almost a fucking week." That was some bad fucking acting, she realized.

"Didn't know you cared." Hanni snarled.

"I should get back to work," Megan said and backed away looking a little shocked. Today she had a chain going across her cheek connecting her nose and ear piercings.

There was a dozen or more people in the restaurant that were more concerned with the drama at the bar than their breakfasts. Gordie had joined Sandra on the hotline, but he was just there for prep. The grey haired lady (who had worked for Spencer's father) had the breakfast under control. The fresh baking smell permeated the restaurant. Scones with raisins and mixed berry muffins were the baking of the day according to the chalkboard by the display case.

"I don't care," Chrys replied to Hanni. "I'm trying to catch a psycho and you're my bait."

"What?" They quickly filled Hanni in on the necklace and Chrys' theory of how the killer was after her. Chrys did her best not to smile.

"Where have you been?" Spencer sat on the backed stool beside her.

"My Aunties." Her voice dropped. "I was freaked out about all the bodies and was tempted to get into my bad habits again. My aunt is a therapist, so I stayed with them a couple days."

Chrys had to admit that was good.

Spencer reached out and rubbed her thigh. He glanced in Jessie's direction to see if she was looking. She wasn't even in the room any more. To Hanni he said, "That's good. But last night you said you were okay."

"I didn't talk to you last night."

"No, you texted me."

"I didn't text you." She put her hands on the bar and fidgeted with her rings. She spun one with an amethyst around her finger. "I haven't been able to find my phone since yesterday afternoon. Last place I saw it was my place … when I went and got a change of clothes."

Spencer took out his phone and quickly went to his text messages. "I have it right here. I texted you asking how you were. You text me back saying you were still shook up. That was last night just before service."

"But I didn't have my phone. Last night I was whining that I wanted my phone. I had my phone before I had a shower then I guess I left my phone somewhere or something because I couldn't find it on my way out. I don't have my phone. Who the hell has my phone?" She looked at both of the Alcrest's and they looked at her with blank expressions.

"What happened to your face and finger?" Hanni didn't ask with concern. Her voice was more that of wanting to thank who did it.

Chrys blinked quickly. "What? Oh I tried slutting around in your heels and fell."

Hanni smirked. "It does take talent."

"I have real tits and an ass, so my balance was off."

"Funny."

For a few minutes Spencer quietly thought of what to do. He picked up his phone and texted Hanni's phone, "When are you coming in?" He slipped the phone back in his pocket. The only person he could think of that would have Hanni's phone was the same guy that talked to him about beets. Would he recognize him if he came into the restaurant? Perhaps he had just been a guy that wanted to talk about how to cook beets and afterward actually went to the booth that sold honey fresh from the hive. Spencer had looked at the booth as he was getting Jessie from the mini doughnuts, but how could he be certain the guy wasn't there? Even seconds after talking to him he couldn't recall what he looked like. He could have been right there in the restaurant. Maybe saying he was going to see about Hanni meant he was going to look for her. Spencer ran a hand through his hair. He was as bad as his sister with her mystery fever.

"I'm going to go walk the dogs then go out. Can I borrow the rental?" Chrys tapped her finger brace on the bar top.

"Where are you going?" Spencer looked at the front door as two men came in. One was in a suit. The other wore a T-shirt and jeans.

"I wouldn't let her."

"Who's asking you, Hanni? Keep your snooty nose out of my business." Chrys took a step toward Hanni who slipped off the bar stool almost stumbling.

Spencer quickly stepped between them. "Cut it out. The last thing we need is you two fighting."

"Are you Spencer Alcrest?" The man in the suit crossed the restaurant in long strides. His hair flowed like chestnut waves and his teeth were bright. He held a microphone in one hand and its chord in the other. The other man was right behind him with a video camera now on his shoulder. "Evan Gage, World News. I was hoping to speak to you and Chrys. You must be Chrys?"

Chrys flashed a smile. "Is this where I say, no comment?"

"Can you put that camera down? What can we do for you?" Spencer noticed the camera never went down.

Evan Gage tapped his man's elbow. A red light suddenly flashed next to the lens of the camera. "You were seen at the Farmers' Market today where Elaine Vogt went missing early this morning. Does this have any connection to the discovery you two made of all the body parts just outside Middleton?"

"What?" Spencer stared at the reporter.

Hanni threw in, "I was there too."

205

"Does her disappearance have something to do with the Wind-Chime Killer?"

"I don't …"

"Is Elaine Vogt his next victim?"

The microphone was put right in Spencer's face. In a second it moved closer to Chrys. Her hand flew up. Her fingers grasped the microphone as her body twisted into the reporter. His wrist bent awkward. The microphone slipped from his grasp. Chrys jumped away from him with the microphone close to her lips. "This just in. You're both fuck-tards."

Spencer's hand went on the lens of the camera pushing the man behind it back. "I said put the camera down. Both of you can leave."

The microphone hit the ground with a thud.

"Come on, Spencer, the Wind-Chime is a big story." Evan Gage pulled up the microphone hand over hand by the chord. "Everyone's looking for a headline. I saw you talking to the detective and thought I saw mine. I won't be the only one to come here."

The camera man backed up to the door before raising the camera again. Gordie stepped around from the kitchen and put himself right in front of the lens. The camera man stepped back at the large sight of the sous chefs' furry face and his back hit the doorframe.

"Don't call me Spencer. You don't know us."

Evan Gage dropped the mic to his side. "Everyone's looking for an edge."

"We're not your edge." Spencer pointed toward the door.

"Other reporters are going to come. I could tell your honest story before they write the wrong story."

"We don't have a story to tell."

The reporter shook his head making his hair do this gentle dance before falling back in place. The camera man held the door open. "Anyone can see you two are involved in this case, whether you can or not. There's a story here and I'll find it. I always do."

"Don't let the door hit your ass on the way out." Chrys walked past them heading to the back.

Spencer nodded at Gordie and watched the big man push his weight against the two men until they were outside.

After giving them a wave Gordie came back in and said, "No seriously, where are all the knives?"

Chapter 31

Bullet waddled across the hardwood floor of the
apartment. The bulldogs front and back halves moved like
a bending spring connected them. Chrys hung the leashes
up next to the door. Breeze ran around her legs a few times
before making a bee-line for the couch, bounced off the
cushion and ran full tilt down the hallway only to come
back and sniff Spencer's feet in the kitchen before grabbing
an empty Powerade bottle and finally settling on the couch.
Bullet sat beside Spencer watching him. The dog's tongue
hung out and dripped onto the floor.

"What are you doing?" Chrys flipped her ankle boots on
the floor and padded across the open room on the balls of
her feet.

Spencer had a few chef knives out on the island
countertop. "The cops wouldn't let me get our knives at the
market, so I'm grabbing my stash. Have you seen the one
from the knife block?"

Chrys pulled the French knife from the inside pocket of
her coat and dropped it on the counter. The 8" blade
stopped spinning with the point facing her brother. "Nope."

"What were you doing with that?"

"There's a psycho on the loose, Spenny. A girl can't be too careful and these aren't exactly guard dogs we have. Can I use the car or not?"

"Where are you going?"

"Just running errands." Chrys knew better than to tell him the truth. She had learned a long time ago how to be a great liar. If she was honest with herself she also knew that he wasn't going to believe her. "What are you going to do?"

"Work. We have lots of prep to do and I want to get all of this psycho stuff out of my head for a while, if I can."

"Must be nice. So you don't need the car then? Can I use it or not?"

"You're not covered under the rental agreement, so be extra careful. No putting your life on the line." Spencer put all of the knives in a plastic tub. A lot of them were not good for constant restaurant use, but they'd have to do for now. "Be careful and don't do anything stupid."

"You know me, brother dear." Chrys' smile disappeared the moment she was away from his gaze. With the plans she had in her head she wasn't sure if she'd come out untouched. She cursed her decision to change into blue jeans when her finger got in the way of pulling up the zipper. She chose a tank-top and then a grey hooded sweatshirt that was pretty baggy. The purpose of the baggy sweatshirt was to hide the final addition to her ensemble. The switchblade Rene Alcrest gave her before he died. He saved it from his time in the Canadian Navy. He told her he hoped she'd never use it, but a young woman needed protection. She hoped she wouldn't need it at all.

"And can you pick up my knives?"

~ * ~

Chrys flinched at the sound of the bell above the door as she moved from the knickknack store into the greenhouse. Before she even stepped completely inside the humid building sweat erupted out of every pore. It was as if she stepped from the Canadian west coast into the South American jungle. The first plants were regular ones you would find in Canada – vegetables, flowers, herbs, though it was what was further on that Chrys was looking for. Tropical plants covered tables along the sides of the long building. They were also down the middle and hanging from the ceiling. The colours went from a vibrant green to almost every other colour you could imagine. The heat pulled the breath from Chrys' lungs. For a moment she felt panic surge through her body until she gasped for air and could settle. There was a generator rumbling that echoed in the tube-like building. The clerk in the store said to go in and she'd find the gardener. She couldn't see anyone.

This wasn't right. Chrys didn't want to be here. She didn't want to go home either, though. What was she going to say to her brother? Here she was following what she could, like O'Donnell told her to, and she wanted to run away before she even found anything.

"Can I help you?"

"Jesus!"

A woman popped her head out from behind a display of plants with large deep green leaves and red flowers. "Did I scare you? You stay in here long enough you forget there's an outside world." She was older, probably in her sixties. She had dirt half-way up her forearms and it was packed

211

under her nails. The craziest thing about her was that each breast seemed to be the size of a regulation soccer ball and they were both packed into a T-shirt. A unicorn tattoo winked at Chrys from on top of one of them. "Is there anything particular you're looking for?"

Did the woman catch her staring? Chrys liked breasts and had played with her share but never anything this big. She made herself concentrate. "Dragon's breath."

The woman's eyebrow went up. "Excuse me?"

"You deal in non-indigenous plants right? Do you have the borrachero tree? Angel's Trumpet flower?" There's no way, right? All the Internet sights said this plant was toxic. It was a hallucinogen. And it wasn't just from the seeds which made scopolamine. She read about a couple of men who made a tea from the blossoms and then amputated each other's penises. Buying this plant couldn't be legal.

The woman said, "Right this way," and headed toward the back of the building.

The greenhouse had a gravel walkway leading from one end to the other on both sides of the middle tables with small paths crossing over every five feet or so. The woman's rubber boots crunched with each step. Chrys' heels slipped between the rocks. There were herbs and flowers and house plants each with their own colour and scent. Chrys pushed a leaf away from her face and swiped at flies. Perspiration stuck to her. She looked over her shoulder. The exit seemed so far away. As she turned back the woman was gone.

Chrys quickly moved down the greenhouse and realized the building was in the shape of an L. The gardener had turned the corner. Chrys slipped two fingers in her jean pocket and fondled the knife handle.

"Here we go. Angel's Trumpet. Are you looking for any particular type or colour?"

The plants were all in pots along the side of the pathway. They stood almost as tall as the two women and then bent over with the flowers dangling beneath. They made Chrys think of someone with dreadlocks. The plants looked like they had been growing upward and then when the flowers bloomed the green stems drooped over so that the trumpet shaped flowers were hanging upside-down. The bottom of the trumpets looked like Marilyn Monroe's dress as the air blew it up. Most of the flowers were white. There were ones that started white at the stem then slowly changed to peach. Some were bright yellow. A couple had orange, red and gold all mixed together like a tequila sunrise. The ones that caught Chrys' eye had magenta around the edges. They were beautiful.

"These are legal?" Chrys was finding it hard to breathe.

"Of course they are. What kind of shop do you think I'm running here?"

"I just mean these plants, they … do you know what they can do?"

"A lot of plants in here are toxic or have some effect if someone does something with them. Guns are perfectly safe until someone loads them and pulls the trigger. A plant by itself is harmless. It's just a plant."

Chrys couldn't disagree with that. The flowers looked beautiful. What else was she supposed to do? "Do you know if anyone bought some of these recently?"

"Not that I can recall. There are a half dozen other greenhouses around the city though that have these flowers. And florists too. Not to mention anyone can get anything

213

online these days. I'm sorry that none of this helps you. Is that everything? I have to get back to work."

"You're not fucking helping me lady!" Chrys spun on the ball of her foot and marched back down the path with the gardener woman yelling at her back about showing respect.

This wasn't working out. Chrys didn't have access to computer databases or geniuses that knew everything about every plant like they did on television. All she had was a crime boss who paid for escorts and a bitch cop that wanted to arrest her.

Chasing the plants was going to be never ending. There were too many avenues which the psycho could have acquired the toxic plant from reputable stores to mail order to driving across the border to Seattle. The guy could have been growing the plant his entire life. Chasing the missing people was pointless. They disappeared in a second like Elaine Vogt with nothing left behind and no witnesses. There one moment and gone the next with no trace.

And what about Elaine Vogt? The police had probably exhausted everything. Hundreds of people were searching around the city. They weren't going to find anything. In reality they should sit back and wait for the body parts to be hung with care; like stockings from the chimney.

O'Donnell said follow what she knew. What did she know? The killer might use scopolamine which was called Devil's Breath and came from the seeds of a plant called Angel's Trumpet which was readily available. He took runaways, hookers and druggies. People who wouldn't really be missed. After doing whatever he did with them he hung their limbs like wind-chimes. He was invisible.

Why Elaine Vogt? She wasn't one of the forgotten. Taking her makes him visible. Frustration? Desperation? Anger?

Chrys sat in the rental car and drummed her fingers on the steering wheel. She absently chewed her bottom lip as the thoughts sprinted through her head.

Hanni?

She couldn't find her phone at home, but Spencer got a text from her. The psycho was in her home. He had the phone. He could have even been in there while she was home. Why didn't he take her? Why would he not take her and snatch some housewife who would be missed. Frustration, desperation, anger and opportunity all rolled into one?

The only thing Chrys knew was that the drug came from the seeds of a flower. Follow the flowers was her only option..

~ * ~

"Pacific Exotics. Sounds lovely." Chrys turned the car off. She had been to four flower shops without finding the Angel's Trumpet in any. She had purposefully left this other greenhouse for last. The front of the wall facing the parking lot was painted with a mural of parrots and macaws flying over a tropical field of flowers. There was a mini-van two cars down from where she parked with the company name written on it and a dumbed down version of the mural.

The building itself was one of those pre-fab domed barn types. The long dome was mostly white with a thick red line over each end. The moment she opened the door she

215

heard something screech. The front of the building had cages with tropical birds in them. A macaw chewed on the wires of its cage. Off to the side were large aquariums. Fish of every colour chased each other around the bubbles and statues of cartoon characters in the pebbly bases. One aquarium had turtles in it. They swam with the current of the water intake, climbed on a rock and dove off the far side to do it all over again. It reminded her of Breeze chasing a ball at the dog park. Down the middle of the store were working water fountains. One was a circle of rocks with a carved mountain on one side that water trickled down. Chrys took a moment to look at the one that resembled a Hawaiian waterfall and smiled at the fountain where the water came out of an elf's penis into a bucket.

"H-hi."

Chrys turned to the man close to her side. He looked to be in his thirties with brown hair and a pleasant face. Spencer said there was nothing special about the man that talked to him at the Farmer's Market. Chrys could say that about this man. She would probably forget his face the moment she walked out. "Hi, do you work here?"

The name tag above his pocket said his name was Aaron. "Y-yes."

"You have flowers don't you?"

He pointed at wide stairs going down just beyond all of the fountains. There was a glass wall at the bottom with a motioned sensor door. "Down there. The climate is different down there."

There were a few people moving around shopping and looking at the aisles of tropical bird and fish food. This was the store you went to when you just didn't have enough to

216

take that trip south. Some workers helped people in the store and in the tropical paradise beyond the glass wall.

"Do you have the Angel's Trumpet flower?"

His eyes scanned the room. "I don't, I don't work with the flowers. Go down the stairs and talk to S-Sam. She can help you."

Chrys gave him a smile and a nod. She couldn't tell if he was intimidated by her or if it was a natural stutter. As she headed down and through the glass door she felt his eyes on her. He could be it. He could be the killer right there. As she heard the door close behind her she took a quick look back. He wasn't there watching her. Maybe she was wrong.

She couldn't believe the change in the air from the other side of the glass wall. She hadn't noticed the lovely cool air conditioning until the moment the automatic door slid closed behind her and sweat appeared on her face. The quick change between cool and hot was worse than the other greenhouse. It made her head spin.

Chrys quickly looked at people with the red Pacific Exotics golf shirt uniforms until she found the name Sam. "Excuse me. I was told by a guy up in the store, shit what was his name? He stuttered. Anyway, he said that you could help me."

Sam smiled as she said, "That would be Aaron." She had jet black hair, wore glasses and had a lot of earrings. "Aaron is, ah," she thought about what she was saying for a moment before changing her mind. "How can I help you?"

"He said you could tell me if you have the Angel's Trumpet flower. He said he didn't know."

"Aaron said that?" Her face scrunched up. "He knows where everything is and especially the brugmansia plants. Right this way."

Again Chrys found herself walking to the back of a greenhouse. "I thought the plant was called borrachero."

"That's more of a slang name for it. Here we have the brugmansia with flowers called Angel's Trumpet. Very toxic, but very beautiful. I don't recommend getting one if you have pets or small children. These are small, but can grow huge. I've heard of ones in the wild that are taller than a house. They are very fragrant, so if you want something that smells great they are a good plant to have." They were in large pots with a lot more leaves than flowers.

Chrys looked back, but couldn't see through the glass wall. "And you said that guy, Aaron, looks after them?"

"He tends to all of the flowers after hours. He makes sure any flowers that drop off go into the garbage so that no children can get to them."

"Ah, thank you." As Chrys walked back toward the store she wondered if Aaron put the fallen flowers into the garbage or into his pocket. From what she had seen on Youtube even just the flower was enough to give you a wild ride.

The air conditioning hit her as she stepped through the glass wall and a chill twisted her entire body. She quickly walked along the aisles but couldn't see him. She had to go tell her brother. This guy seemed weak, but that didn't mean anything. From what she knew with the scopolamine powder he could make the biggest man do what he wanted.

"D-did you find what you were looking for?"

The car keys fell out of Chrys' hand, bouncing off her foot onto the ground. The guy was there by her car waiting for her. How would he know what car was hers unless he had been around The Alcrest.

"I'll get those." Aaron quickly got down on his knees and snatched the ring of keys from the ground. As he put them in her hand he said, "Have a nice day," with a strange smile.

Chapter 32

"Did you hear they found body parts?"

Chrys was just walking into the restaurant and hadn't even shut the service door to the restaurant behind her. "What?"

Izzy took dirty glasses and mugs from her tray and put them next to the dishpit sink. She had her red hair pinned up except for the bangs that hung around her face. "It was on the radio. They found body parts while looking for that woman that went missing this morning."

"Was it her?" Chrys slid the box of knives onto the back prep table. "Was it the housewife? Where's Spencer and Hanni?"

"They're in the dining room. The radio didn't say who the body parts belonged to. They said the search continues though. That has to mean something."

Mr. O sat at his table by the window in the dining room. A large group had three tables pushed together. They were finishing their lunch. Spencer sat at a far table with papers covering it. Hanni was across from him playing with her nails.

"Chrys," Jessie gently touched her arm before she could walk past. "Can you start at 6:00 pm tonight? We don't have reservations until half-past. Izzy is going to take a couple hours break then come back to do Hanni's shift."

"Why can't she do her shift?"

Jessie looked down at the reservation book. She didn't seem to want to look across the dining room at the table she, herself, and Spencer would often share. "She says she's still not ready."

"She's so full of shit she makes a port-a-potty look clean. What does she think she's going to do if she's not working? She can't go anywhere with this guy out there."

"Go ask her."

Gordie leaned out of the kitchen entry. "You get our knives, Chrys?"

"They're in the back, Gordie."

Chrys headed across the dining room. She wasn't sure how she was going to do what was in her head. All she knew was that she had to keep the bitch close. "What are you doing?"

Spencer didn't look up. "Food costing."

"I'm not talking to you."

Hanni looked up from her nails. "What?"

"You're not working tonight, so what are you doing?"

"She's going to stay up in our apartment," Spencer answered for her.

The expression across Hanni's face said she was not too happy about that plan. "And what do you want me to do up there? I'm not laying on the couch watching your spaghetti westerns all night."

"You'll be safe. We still don't know if this guy is after you or not." It looked like Spencer had new worry lines on

222

his face. Every time the bell above the door sounded he looked and almost jumped to his feet. He might have invited a serial killer to dinner, but that didn't mean he wouldn't come earlier.

"Nobody's after me."

"Somebody's using your phone to answer my texts."

"Somebody might have my phone, but the rest is just her imagination."

"Screw you." Chrys sat down between the two of them.

Hanni licked her lips. "Fine, I'll stay upstairs, but I need to go home and get some clothes."

"No you don't. You can wear Chrys' clothes. Right?"

Chrys shook her head. "I don't want her skank disease in my clothes."

"Look at her big ass. I'll swim in her pants."

Chrys snarled. "My ass is perfect. You wish you had an ass like mine. And while we're at it, why don't we mention how you won't fill out my shirts either."

"Your tits aren't much bigger than mine."

"Still bigger!"

"Ladies!" Spencer slammed his hands down on the table. A couple papers fluttered to the floor. "Cut it out. You both have to deal with this."

Chrys crossed her arms in front of her. "Why?"

"Hanni is our friend. And she's part of my life now. You're going to have to deal with it."

The two women glared at each other. They both were having the same thought from different sides.

"Spence," Hanni ran her finger around the top of her wine glass. "We had sex. We're not buying matching robes."

The bell above the door rang making Spencer flinch. Detective Washburn stepped inside and spoke to Jessie before being pointed in their direction.

Spencer turned to Hanni only she wouldn't look at him. What did she mean? He had never been one of those people to have a relationship just for sex. Was that all she wanted? Was he that much of a fool? Could he be okay with that? He didn't want marriage or anything serious, so why not? He hated it when his sister might be right.

"Am I interrupting?" Wash had her hands in her pockets. She didn't look as angry as she did a few hours before. She just looked tired.

"No," Spencer's voice dropped, "It's nothing important. Have a seat."

"I can't stay. I wanted to talk to you." She nodded at Chrys. Wash's voice was rather somber. "I wanted to tell you we found Crystal Stone. Her arms at least. We identified her through fingerprints. We also found lower legs which we believe are Stanley Haul's. And thanks to your information about scopolamine we might have a suspect."

"Who?" Chrys slid forward on her chair.

Wash's blond hair seemed to wave as she shook her head. "You know I can't tell you that."

"If this was a mystery novel you'd tell me."

"Well this isn't a mystery novel, now is it?"

"Where did you find the body parts?"

Wash took a breath. "Tulloch Park on the edge of city limits. It looked like their limbs had been hung there for a few days. A group searching for Elaine Vogt found them. They were hanging in amongst some evergreens with Crystal Stone's head in the middle."

Hanni put a hand over her mouth and closed her eyes tight.

Spencer let out a sigh of relief. "So nothing connected to us then." He felt a little ill to be happy about that.

"What about Elaine?"

"Nothing yet. I have to get back out there."

"Thank you, Detective." Spencer stared at his sister.

"I'm going to have patrolmen outside. We still don't know who this guy is."

"Thank you." Spencer kept his eyes on his sister. He was afraid if he looked at the detective she would see something in him.

"Do you think he'll come after us?" Chrys asked.

Wash shrugged. "Spencer's truck. The Farmer's Market. He might. Stay safe. Stay around each other." She gave them a nod before heading for the door.

Even with all this going on in the outside world life continued in the restaurant. The large group was leaving. Gordie was replacing the upstairs collection of knives with the now sharp yellow handled restaurant quality blades. Jessie dealt with payments as Izzy cleared the remaining dishes from the three tables. Life continued on no matter what was happening.

"I need to get clothes," Hanni said again with her arms crossed and fingers drumming.

Tonight they had an Aboriginal rapper in, Johnny Cee, performing so they still had to move some tables around to try and get room for more people. Spencer wasn't sure what kind of a crowd they were going to get. He was a big champion of diversity and local talent, so here it was. Country last weekend, rap this weekend. Rap and swearing was not their usual entertainment (Johnny Cee had filled in

225

as a dishwasher for them a few times), so maybe it was a good thing to have a police car sitting out on the street. Spencer didn't think there would be any trouble, but didn't mind the deterrent.

Spencer took a deep breath before speaking. "Okay, Hanni, if you insist on getting some clothes and stuff I'll take you."

Chrys couldn't let Hanni out of her sight. "Why don't I take her?"

"No, it's not safe."

"Come on, Spenny, the cops are everywhere, this guy is probably long gone. And you're both right. I have been blowing things way out of proportion. My imagination took over and I saw things that weren't there." From the look on her brother's face she wasn't convincing him. "We're going to be busy tonight and you need to be here to help prep for it. You know that. I'm just trying to help."

"I know that Chrys. Thank you."

Sucker!

"Hanni," Spencer's voice was soothing this time, "Do you mind if Chrys goes with you to get your things?"

Hanni looked at him with a blank expression. "I don't care. Let's just get this over with."

~ * ~

"What are you doing?"

Chrys was out of the car before Hanni was able to step out. "I'm going with you."

"I think I can get my clothes on my own."

"Like I really want to go in your hovel again. I'm not here for you." Chrys stomped beside Hanni. She looked up

226

and down the street without knowing what she was looking for. This psycho was like air. Spencer was face to face with him, maybe, and couldn't recall what he looked like afterward. At least there was no sign of the guy from the greenhouse. "Let's do this quick."

Hanni growled at her. "You guys are worried over nothing.

"How'd the nut-job get your phone then?"

"I could have dropped it anywhere and who says he has it?"

"Oh my God, you suck." Chrys slipped her fingers in her jeans pocket. The switchblade was still there waiting. Her fingertips caressed the wrinkled handle. "Think about it. You had your phone before your shower and couldn't find it after your shower. You really don't get it, do you? He was in your place while you were showering."

Hanni stared at her for a long moment before slipping the key in the lock. She said, "You're paranoid," but her voice said she was scared.

Chrys didn't know what to expect. Her free hand closed into a tight fist. She took another look around as the blond pushed the door open and then stepped inside. Chrys slipped the knife from her pocket and held it behind her leg. Her thumb was ready to push the button and pop the sharp blade out. Chrys held her breath as she stepped inside.

"Wait here and I'll grab some things," Hanni walked toward the back.

"You sure you don't want me to come with you?"

Hanni spun around. "Maybe you can help. Would your brother like me in a black bustier, garter and stocking combo or a simple pail blue baby-doll teddy?"

Chrys' face scrunched up with disgust. "Where's your bathroom?"

"Down the hall."

The house apartment was much cleaner than Chrys' room in the apartment above The Alcrest. She glanced in the bedroom as she passed. Hanni was folding clothes and putting them in a large bag. The bathroom door was closed. Chrys squeezed the knife in her hand. He could be in there waiting for them. Her heart pounded in her chest. She felt blood pulse through her temples. She turned the handle and pushed the door.

Her phone vibrated against her chest.

"Fuck!" Her thumb twitched. The blade swung out of the knife handle with a thwak making Chrys jump again. "Jesus."

"What the hell?"

Chrys switched the knife to her other hand and hid it behind her leg as she turned to Hanni. "Sorry. My phone vibrated and it startled me.

"Jesus, Chrys. Stop living in your dream world." Before Hanni went back in the bedroom she called out. "Grab my toothbrush and shampoo … never mind. I'll get it myself. Just tell me when you're done."

Chrys put the knife blade back in the handle and took her cell phone out from insider her bra. It had the usual boob smear across the screen. Spencer wanting to know if they were okay. Really?

There were "show" towels on a bar on the wall. The matt in front of the toilet, the lid cover and a matt by the bathtub were all the same blue colour as the cloud covered shower curtain which was closed. Shampoo, conditioner and gel shaving cream were all lined up in the corner.

228

Chrys did her thing before going to the sink. All of Hanni's make-up was in a caddy instead of spread around like Chrys'.

"Where's your toothbrush," Chrys called out.

"In the shower," was the response that came back.

The shower curtain was spread out blocking the tub and shower. Who closed their curtain? All the movies Chrys had ever seen with someone hiding behind a shower curtain flashed through her head. But this was no movie. She got the knife out and pressed the button. The blade swung out and locked in place. This time she heard her heart pounding. She reached up with her other hand. Everything was moving in slow motion. She held her breath.

With one swift pull she yanked the curtain and jumped back. Nothing. Nothing but a tile wall. What the hell?

"I grabbed your brushes too," Chrys said as she dropped everything into Hanni's hands.

"You're all sweaty."

"Let's just get out of here."

Chapter 33

The Alcrest's think they're the winners. They've found my collection, they've been to my home. They think they know me. All of us together is a coincidence, but now they vex me.

They'll be my end game. Grandpa was no one. He killed and killed and nobody knows who he was because a man named Ted Bundy took his thunder. Everyone's going to know me. I'll be more famous that he ever was. People will know my picture when they see it. I've been nothing in my life, but I'll be notorious in their death.

I watch the cars pull into the back parking lot of their den and realize they don't see me. I could walk up to them and take them one by one and they would never be able to tell the police who I was. A shadow. A wisp of wind. The boogeyman. Nobody.

They will know me soon. There are stories in the news, but nobody yet knows me.

I step from the van and walk toward the restaurant. The Chef was just outside smoking. He isn't a smoker. I've been watching him a while and this is something brand new. Something against his character. I've done that to him. I'm the cause.

You know, it's the cocky ones who are the most unsafe. Nothing bad would ever happen to them.

I knock on the upstairs door. My hand is in the baggy in my pocket. This isn't a blown kiss time. The door opens.

"Yeah?"

She's something up close. She's wearing shorts and a T-shirt which hugs everything. I can feel her scream inside me. No time for that now.

"If you're looking for Spencer or Chrys they're downstairs."

I grab her arm with one hand. The other rams a full hand of the powder into her nose and mouth. She's had white powder up her nose before. Her hand grabs my wrist. I push her inside. Dogs bark. The door closes behind me. She sucks in the powder. She falls and I watch her twist on the floor. There's no stopping it. In seconds she won't have a choice. She's mine.

"Sit in this chair."

Hanni sits down in the dining room chair I've placed in line with the door leading down to the Alcrest. Her eyes are like glass. This wasn't my first plan. Why should I be the killer?

"Take this knife." It was nice of the Chef to have a bin of knives sitting on the kitchen island.

Her fingers wrap around the handle. Her eyes never move. I know this phase. She'd eat her own flesh if I told her to.

"If anyone comes through that door I want you to run across the room screaming and then I want you to stab them to death." I press my lips against her temple. Blood drips from her nose to her lips and she doesn't move. She is so mine. I only wish I would be up here to see her kill one of them. I've directed the scene and now it is time to let the actors take over.

Chapter 34

Spencer threw his dirty apron onto a table right next to a "Reserved" sign before slumping into a chair with his back to the wall. It had been a successful night financially. Johnny Cee had brought in a crowd that spent a lot on drinks and little on food. A group in the frame room bought appetizer after appetizer as they played the game Betrayal at the House on the Hill. Surprisingly it was the board game group they had to ask to keep the noise down. The rapper sang a few songs to loud cheers. Some people didn't like the cursing. Spencer didn't care. That was the point of singer/songwriter night and the point of the restaurant. People had to be free to express themselves.

He smiled at Izzy as she handed an order across the pass. There were still a few late tables that his team could handle.

"What the fuck, Spenny?" Chrys flopped into a chair. Chits slipped out of her billfold.

"What?" She scrunched up her nose at her brother's expression. "I can take a break to you know."

"That's not what I meant. I meant this," she hit the reserved sign with the finger brace. "Where is he?"

"Maybe the beet guy wasn't the psycho. Maybe he doesn't have the phone. I can't make someone come here." He couldn't make customers come consistently, so how could he make a man who did a fine job of not being seen show up? "I should go check on Hanni."

"Chef, may I?" Izzy bounced beside the table. Her red hair slapped the sides of her face.

"What's up?"

Izzy was the youngest of the serving staff. She joined the team when everyone else was jumping ship. "Table thirteen would like to buy you and the kitchen crew a drink. They've been sitting here a while and said you guys have been working hard."

Spencer let his head turn to see the table. It was an older couple. He gave them a wave. "Find out what everyone wants."

"What about you?"

"I don't know."

"Get him a tequila," Jessie slipped into another empty chair. "What are we talking about?"

Chrys glared at her with a resting bitch face. She pulled her phone from her bra and wiped the screen with a napkin.

"The killer and where he is. I thought he'd come here." Spencer rubbed his head.

"Do you really want him here?" Jessie put her hand on his arm.

He played with his apron strings. On the plus side he wasn't thinking about the numbers all night and the drink Izzy put down in front of him was the first alcoholic drink he had in a couple days. After a sip he said, "Guess he's too busy playing with Elaine Vogt."

236

"No, he's not." Chrys passed her phone across the table. "Says right there Elaine Vogt was found an hour ago walking in Tulloch Park. We have to call Wash." She looked at her brother with wide eyes and her tongue between her teeth.

"I have to go see about Hanni."

"Fuck Hanni! Everyone else does."

"Chrys! Stop it."

Jessie stood up quickly. "I'll go check on Hanni."

"I'll go with you so I can change." As Chrys pushed her chair back it almost tipped.

"Don't you still have tables to clear? What are you changing for?"

Chrys stared down at her brother. "My tables are pretty well clean." Three of her tables still had the remnants of dinner or dessert on them, but all of her customers were gone. "And if we're going to see Wash I don't want to smell like red wine and Alfredo sauce."

"I'll be right back." Jessie walked toward the back trying to hide her smile.

"We're not going to see Detective Washburn. I'm sure she's busy."

Chrys sat back down. "Don't be a dick."

"Chrys, I said no. She won't talk to us anyway. Maybe I'll give her a call in the morning."

Chrys groaned as she got back up and marched away. She slipped her phone back into the left cup of her bra. As soon as she found someone who sewed she was going to go ahead with her idea for brassieres with phone pockets. All she had to do was get around the possibilities of phones leading to breast cancer.

She scooted around the lady from table thirteen outside the bathroom. The guy in the dishpit was putting glassware through.

Chrys opened the door which lead to the stairs going up to the apartment. The light flicked in the stairwell. At least it was inside and not out in the elements. As the bottom door closed she heard a banging at the top. Wood on wood. There was a lump at the top of the stairs. Chrys took the steps two at a time using the railing to pull herself up. The lump was reaching up to the door handle. It opened slightly and banged shut. Jessie's fingers struggled to hang onto the door handle as it opened again and she pulled it back.

Chrys was three steps away. The light went bright. There was red on the door handle. Jessie's fingers slipped off as the door yanked open. A knife.

With a step and jump Chrys was over the body on the top landing. Both hands grabbed the wrist holding the knife. She turned her shoulder and hit the person as she stumbled into the room.

"Hanni?" Chrys' voice cracked.

Hanni pulled her arm back. Maybe it was the surprise, but Chrys' grip loosened. There was something in the blond woman's eyes. She had one purpose.

"Hanni stop it."

The knife came down in an over hand arch as a scream erupted from Hanni's larynx.

Chrys stepped to the side. She felt the wind from the arm and knife as it narrowly missed its mark. It was one of Spencer's chef knives – 10 inches long and as sharp as it could get. Her body twisted as her kickboxing training took over and she slammed a fist into Hanni's side. Pain lightninged from her fractured finger and up her forearm.

Before the other woman could recover Chrys let her stomach muscles torque her body the other way. Her open left hand connected with Hanni's face. She felt her nose and mouth beneath her palm.

Blood erupted from Hanni's nostril. It dripped over her lips which turned into a snarl. She thrust forward, the knife tip aimed directly at Chrys' chest.

Chrys was too late to block it. Her body had quarter turned when the blade connected just above her left breast. She screamed. She heard a crack and felt pain and pressure against her chest. Her hand connected with Hanni's wrist. The knife broke free and twirled across the room. Blood sprayed out from the blade as it spun.

Oh God, Jessie.

Hanni screamed. She flailed at Chrys with her razor-like fingernails.

Chrys let out her own scream as the long nails tore into her chin. She lowered her head and slammed her shoulder against the other woman like a linebacker taking out a quarterback. Her arms wrapped around the thin woman. Chrys pushed her backward. Hanni hit and scratched at her back. They hit the island. Chrys stepped back and flew punch after punch into Hanni's stomach. Pain vibrated up her one arm.

She stopped the moment Hanni slumped down onto her knees. Tears flowed down the blonds cheeks. Blood continued to trickle out of her nose. "Stop," was all Hanni repeated between moans. One arm wrapped around her stomach. The other rested over one of the chairs.

Chrys stumbled back a few steps, her breath coming quick, before turning around. She had to check on Jessie. All she knew was that there was blood.

The warriors yell made her turn back. Hanni pulled knives from the box on the island, one in each hand. She held them out at her sides. Her scream was followed by a snarl. Her bare feet padded on the floor as she charged across the room.

Without a thought Chrys let out a scream and ran toward the other woman. She had done this move before in high school and again in roller derby. It had to be done quickly or she'd feel both blades. Her shoulder speared Hanni's abdomen. Her arms wrapped around the woman's long legs as she lifted her into the air.

Hanni brought the blades down.

Chrys dove toward the floor. There was a thud and a crack as they hit. She heard a strange noise come out of Hanni and metal hit the floor on either side. Chrys' own head hit the floor sending fireworks in front of her eyes. It was different without a helmet. She wasn't going to recover easy.

What if Hanni was still ready to fight? She wanted to kill Chrys.

Where were the knives?

Jessie?

Chrys pushed herself up. Hanni was half up, her face was turned toward her. Her eyes were open. Chrys torqued her body again. Her left fist flew out directly on target. The blonde's hair twisted around her face as she dropped to the side, her face now covered in blond locks. Chrys' weight made her flop down on top of her.

"Okay world, stop spinning." Chrys rose to a half sitting position. She wasn't certain how long she had been out. Seconds? Minutes? She put two fingers on Hanni's neck, blood pulsed beneath the skin. "Why did you do this?"

Chrys pulled her cell phone out of her bra. Pieces fell to the floor and onto the body underneath her. "Why?"

As she got to her feet her knees felt like they were ready to give in. It reminded her of seeing a horse's first steps. Her head spun as pain speared her brain. Something wet and sticky draped down over one eye and as she breathed in her chest hurt. Her shoulder wasn't too good either.

She stumbled toward the stairs. If the crazy bitch came after Chrys again she wasn't sure what she'd do. The hit to the floor took a lot out of her. The world was a funhouse. The cordless phone was on the coffee table. As she picked it up she kicked one of the knives under the couch. She glanced back. Hanni was still motionless on the floor.

Chrys was already listening to the phone ringing as she went down to her knees at the doorway. Jessie had held on long enough to keep the door closed either trying to stop Hanni from finishing her off or to stop her from going downstairs.

"Thank you for calling The Alcrest Gastropub, this is Spencer. How can I help you?"

Chrys put her fingers on Jessie's neck. "Come … up … stairs." She didn't realize she was crying until that moment. The back of her hand wiped at one eye. As she held it in front of her she saw it was covered in crimson. "Call … nine-one … one. Jessie." The phone clicked off. Two seconds later the basement door opened and Chrys was able to slump against the doorframe. Everything seemed to be getting dark around the edges.

Chapter 35

"Stay there. Give me a minute. Fuck. Come here."

"Can you make up your mind?" Spencer pushed the curtain aside as he stepped in where his sister sat on a hospital bed. He quickly pulled it closed behind him.

Chrys had been able to push the paper gown off, but found herself stuck. She sat on the edge of the bed with her arm across her bare chest covering what she didn't want her brother to see. Her left breast had bandages on it with wrap going around her neck and under her arm. The bruising went out from under the bandages in a variety of purples and dark greens. She had a cut above her eye which had been sewn shut. Hard blue threads stuck out. There were more cuts on her face from Hanni's fingernails which didn't require bandages.

They weren't fingernails. They were claws.

"My shirt's all bloody and I can't get it on."

"I brought you a sweatshirt." Spencer held up a grey hooded sweatshirt with the space ship Serenity on it. Chrys loved her oversized sweats. "Turn around and I'll put it on you."

Chrys stood up and did as she was asked. She had more scrapes on her back. The bandage on the side of her abdomen was where one of the knives had sliced her as she speared Hanni. "Where were the dogs? They weren't there when I got to the apartment. Are they -" The sweatshirt was lowered over her head.

"They're fine. They were in the bedroom. Remember Hanni asked if they could be put in there before we left her alone?"

Getting one arm down a sleeve she turned to her brother. "And Jessie, how is she?"

"In surgery. It looks like she was able to block some of the attack but she still took a stab to the chest. Where's Sloane? I thought she was here."

"She went to get the car. I told her I want to get out of here. I've been in this hospital enough this week. Where's Hanni?"

Spencer crossed his arms in front of him. "In another room with Detective Washburn. They are pretty sure she was drugged with scopolamine. They pumped her stomach. She probably won't remember a thing." He looked out the window. It was almost morning and seemed like it was going to be a nice day as far as the weather went. Inside him he knew that even though Hanni was drugged he didn't know if others would welcome her back. It was like his truck with body limbs in it. She would not remember what she did but everyone else would. Especially Jessie. Assuming Jessie was going to survive. "I have to get back upstairs."

"I guess we know why the psycho didn't show, eh? Is Hanni alright otherwise? Did he do anything to her?"

He sighed. "She has cracked ribs, a concussion, bruises everywhere, but I'm guessing that was all you. They've taken off the restraints they had her in when she first got here, so that's something. What did you do to her anyway?"

"Remember how I took down Tits McGee at the West Coast Roller Classic last year? Same thing. Without helmets."

"Ouch." Spencer gave his sister a hug then backed away when she groaned. "Go home and get some rest. Izzy took the dogs, so don't worry about them. Tell Gordie I probably won't be there today."

"Keep us posted on Jessie. Oh, my cell phone got trashed, so call me on the house phone."

"Will do." Spencer gave her a kiss on the side of her forehead. Last summer it had been his turn with the injuries and he knew nowhere on her body was going to feel good. Everything probably hurt. He squeezed her hand slightly before heading out.

"Spence."

"Yeah?" He popped his head back through the curtain.

"This is, like, totally off topic, but did your parents ever tell you anything about my parents?"

His face scrunched up. It had been a long time since Chrys mentioned anything about her past before the Alcrest's. He could still remember the day she came into their lives as a foster child. "No. Why are you asking?"

"No reason. Must have been a dream I was having."

~ * ~

245

"This didn't hurt as much last night." Chrys found it hard to move her arms to the side to pull herself out of the car seat and using her stomach muscles to just stand up was a task in itself.

Sloane took her by the hand and steadied her with the other as they worked together to get Chrys out of the car. "Your adrenaline's not pumping any more. Get terrified again and I bet you'll be able to lift a house."

"I wasn't terrified." Sloane stopped until Chrys looked at her. "What? I wasn't."

"Right. A crazed woman is trying to cut you up and you weren't afraid."

"I didn't have the time to. Hi guys."

Gordie looked up from the spider he had been watching on the ground. He flicked his spent cigarette into the closest puddle. "Hey, it's Kung Fu Panda. How you feeling?" Gordie scratched his beard. He was still in street clothes, his ball cap with a gold dollar sign on solid black was turned so the bill was over one eye.

"Sore and tired. What are you doing here so early?" Chrys stopped and leaned herself against her girlfriend.

"Spencer called me in since he's not here. Is everyone else okay?" He nodded as he was filled in about the other women. "So how good did it feel to throw a beat down on Hanni?"

Chrys kept her lips closed tight. She had to look up to avoid cracking under the others gaze. "Do you have anything for pain?"

"Are you talking to me?"

Chrys looked back at Gordie. "Yeah. Do you have any of your stuff on you? Something that might help take the

246

pain away or at least mellow it out?" She looked back up under the wooden stairs leading to their apartment.

"I do, but I was saving it for my walk home after work."

"What's that?" Chrys poked her nose upward. Hanging from a nail or something beneath the second floor landing was a plastic bag.

"An empty dime bag?"

"Funny guy."

"Better shut up about that, mate." Sloane directed their attention to the silver convertible pulling into the lot.

Detective Washburn spoke as she got out of her car. "Chrys, I tried catching you at the hospital but you left before I could. I wanted to check in with you about last night. How are you feeling?"

Gordie said, "I'm getting to work," as he quickly went inside.

Chrys stopped leaning against Sloane. She wanted to appear stronger than she felt at the moment. "Like I got in a cat fight where the other cat had knives for claws. Are you arresting Hanni?"

"I don't think we'll be pressing charges. I wish we could find out how she got drugged though. Your brother said Hanni was with you up until you started working. Did you notice any differences in her behavior?" The detective's eyes were always on. She looked everywhere.

"You mean like psychotic homicidal tendencies?" Chrys could have been nicer to the police detective. She could have, but didn't want to.

"You didn't see anyone else?"

Chrys shook her head. The cop actually looked more tired than Chrys felt. Tired, but still good. Good hair, good body, good legs, nice shoes. Fuck her. "How's that woman that he took from the market?"

Wash put her hands in the pockets of her leather jacket. "She's at the hospital too. A couple of kids who drove down a bush road in Tulloch Park saw her in their headlights. She was completely naked and had been walking through the woods for who knows how long. Her feet were all cut up. Her body had lacerations from the trees. And of course she doesn't know what happened."

"Why didn't he kill her?"

"If I knew that I'd be one step closer to catching him. Well, I wanted to make sure you were okay and you are. The lab guys might have left a mess upstairs. Sorry about that." Detective Washburn gave the two women a nod before backing away.

"Wash," Chrys didn't want to say anything, however she had also been through enough on her own. Her brother was right. The excitement of hunting down killers wasn't worth all the pain, emotional and physical. She may not be able to stop them from coming after them, but she could certainly not go looking for them. "I might have a suspect." She waited for Wash to look back at her with raised eyebrows before continuing. "There's a guy named Aaron at Pacific Exotics. They deal with exotic art, animals and plants. They have the plant that you can make scopolamine from. This Aaron guy knows about it and he creeped me out when I was there. It might be nothing."

"I'll check him out. Get some rest."

"What day is it?" Chrys asked after the detective's car was gone.

"Sunday," Sloane stated.

Chrys walked to the stairs, grabbed onto the railing and carefully took a step up. "This has been one long fucking weekend." With Sloane's hand on the small of her back she felt like she could get up easier. Her mind twisted with the possibilities of what happened last night. Could the psycho have been in the apartment when she and Hanni got back from getting her things? No, the dogs were still out and would have gone nuts. He had to get in through the same door they were headed towards. Did he blow Hanni a kiss the moment she opened the door or did he overpower her first? How would he carry the powder?

As they reached the top landing she dropped down to her knees.

"What are you doing? Are you okay?"

Chrys let out a moan. "I have to get that baggie that's under here. I think it might be a clue."

"Alright, Velma, I'll climb down and get it. You stay up here and look for Scooby."

Chrys smacked Sloane's backside as the tattooed woman maneuvered to climb beneath the landing. She pulled herself up seconds later with the empty bag. Gordie was right. It was a sandwich baggie. It had a white dust residue inside.

"This is it." Chrys stepped inside the apartment. "This is proof of what he did." Her brain was suddenly distracted by what her eyes saw. "Wash wasn't kidding. They didn't clean up shit." There was fingerprint dust up and down the doorframe. Chrys and Hanni's blood was still on the living room floor. "Jessie's blood is probably on the stairs. I have to clean it before my brother …"

"You have to go to bed." Sloane carefully took Chrys by the shoulders and pointed her in the direction of the

249

hallway and bedrooms. "I'll clean up. You need your rest."

Chapter 36

The doorbell rang.

Chrys looked down from the vast staircase. She ran down three steps before sitting on the polished bannister and riding down the rest of the way. She was twelve and in a sundress with shorts hidden underneath. The doorbell rang.

Chrys sat up in her bed and moaned with pain. She had been having such a nice dream about her childhood and stuff that wasn't her childhood at the same time. Now she was in reality in her messy room. Balls of lava moved in the lamp on her dresser in a delicate dance. Her television was off. The game controller was still on her chest. She had tried playing a little Tomb Raider when she got into bed, however her eyes didn't stay open long. She reached for her phone to check the time. It took a second to remember what had happened to it.

The doorbell rang followed by knocking.

She wasn't sure how long she had been asleep. Sloane was obviously gone and her brother likely wasn't back.

She stumbled down the hallway. As she reached for the doorknob a single thought came to the forefront of her mind. What if the psycho killer was there on the other side? Did killers ring doorbells? Chrys braced herself, not sure how much of a fight she'd be able to give. She turned the deadbolt. One fist was raised and ready. She suddenly wished she had put shoes on. Bare feet were not as effective as three inch heels.

She turned the doorknob and took a jump back. The door swung open. On the other side stood a tall man in a dark suit with his hands folded in front of him.

"Glenn?" Chrys took a breath. "It's not Monday is it?"

"No, Miss Alcrest." A pleasant musky smell came in the door. "Mr. O'Donnell wanted me to deliver this to you. He says when you watch it to start at 7:00pm last night and asks that you don't get mad. He has this for good reasons." Glenn held out one hand with a USB stick between thumb and finger.

As soon as Chrys took it the driver headed down the stairs. She stared at the tinted windows of the black town-car running in the parking lot below wondering if the man himself was in the back seat as it drove away.

"Let's see what we have here." Chrys shut and locked the door before turning around.

Sloane had done a fine job of scrubbing the blood from the floor. You would never know a battle of life and death had happened in the same room. Spencer's laptop was not on the living room table like it usually was. Things had been so screwy lately that he could have it anywhere. There was a computer downstairs in his office. Lunch serves was over, such as it was on a Sunday, so it wouldn't be too busy down there. And Spencer could have come back and stayed down there to not disturb her or might still be at the hospital. If O'Donnell wanted her to see whatever was on the USB then it had to be worth something.

She wore grey sweatpants with EFDS (Elizabeth Frances Dance Studio) across her behind and the hoodie her brother had brought her this morning. Not exactly restaurant attire, but neither were the bandages and bruises. She slipped into her ankle boots and headed down the inside stairs. Jessie's blood stain had not lifted so well. Her adrenaline was flowing again.

"Chrys, you're up." Gordie was scrubbing a pot at the dishpit sink. He quickly reached up and turned down the music.

"Spencer here?"

"No." He followed Chrys into the office. "I sent the dishwasher home. Lunch was really slow, so Ranger, Mallory and I have been taking turns with the dishes."

Chrys sat behind her brother's desk and plugged the USB into the computer. She looked up at Gordie. "Why are you telling me?"

"It's your restaurant, right?"

She didn't know what to say to that. She wondered what Spencer would say. She took the mouse and clicked on the USB file which popped up on the monitor. It was a video file. "Any word on Jessie?"

"Last I heard she was in surgery." Gordie returned to the dishes. Rap music came out of the speakers above the machine.

Chrys clicked on the video file with yesterday's date. The moment she double clicked on it a picture of the parking lot behind The Alcrest Gastropub appeared on the monitor. O'Donnell had a surveillance camera on the back of their restaurant. Why? Where was it? It had most of the parking lot with the back stairs in the center. She watched for a few moments as Sandra arrived early in the morning and Spencer stepped out and got into Jessie's car to go to the fish market. Why the hell was O'Donnell watching the restaurant? She could talk to him about it at a later date.

She skipped through time stopping at 7:00pm. She recognized Jessie's yellow bug, Hanni's car, Spencer's rental and a couple other cars in the parking lot. A car pulled into the lot and a man and woman climbed out of the sedan and headed around the building toward the front door. A van turned into the parking lot at the farthest entrance and parked behind a pick-up. It was barely within view of the camera. The driver got out and walked straight toward the stairs. Chrys watched his back. There was nothing really special about him. Average height and size, dark clothes, absolutely nothing distinctive. He looked around before running up the stairs and knocking on the apartment door. A minute later it opened. The camera was high up so she could see Hanni over the man's shoulder.

They were speaking. What were they saying? Within seconds the man pulled his hand from his pocket. He shoved it in Hanni's face. Her hands flailed grabbing to gain balance. Her back hit the doorframe. She hit and scratched at his hands.

She put up a fight, Chrys realized. Maybe the girl had spunk after all. It had to be then that the baggie fell out of his pocket.

Hanni's hands dropped to her sides. The man said something in her ear, she turned disappearing inside, and he followed her into the apartment. The door shut. Almost forty-five minutes later the door opened again and he stepped out by himself. He ran down the stairs and walked quickly to the van. This time he wore a baseball cap, an Alcrest one. It must have been one of Spencer's. He didn't raise his head. His shoulders were slumped forward, chin down to his chest, hands in his pockets, as he moved quickly toward his van.

Back in high school there had been guys who moved the same way as he was. They weaved in and out of everyone else never really being noticed and wishing they wouldn't be seen. The less they were noticed, the less they were picked on.

Chrys clicked pause at the moment he was about to walk around his van. It was the closest he was to the camera. He had dark hair and glasses. He looked like you wouldn't suspect him of doing anything wrong. He was one of those people who got picked on, not one who controlled others. He was the kind of predator that needed a powder to make his victims do what he wanted. He was weak.

It was the van Chrys' eyes focused on. It was barely visible, but there was something like pink flowers on the back of it. She knew that van.

"Oh shit. I sent her to the wrong place." She pushed out of the chair and left the office. Gordie wasn't washing dishes any more. She stormed through the hallway and started digging through the hostess stand as soon as she reached the main restaurant. "Anybody see Jessie's keys? Nobody moved her stuff, right?"

"She usually just chucks them in the top." Ranger looked in and instantly found them. He kept his eyes away from Chrys' gaze. He was just like the man in the video. Silent, hidden away in his own shell. She wondered if Ranger had evil thoughts.

"You going somewhere?" Gordie took up the entire entry to the kitchen.

"To a flower shop." Chrys grabbed three dinner rolls off the bread table on her way out the back door.

~ * ~

Chrys groped herself for the third time and wished she had her cellphone. She should have called Spencer, before driving across the city, and told him what her plan was. He would have tried to talk her out of going. She could have called Wash and told her about the video and what she saw. That would have brought up questions about O'Donnell and why he had the restaurant under surveillance and she probably would have been sidetracked. She planned on finding out about the gangster's intentions herself. For now she should have listened to the detective and stayed out of this. What she was doing was stupid. But then, why break with tradition?

As the front of the Volkswagen edged past the corner of the building her eyes caught site of a mini-van parked down beside the long greenhouse. She suddenly wished she wasn't in a bright yellow "punch-buggy." The van had the business name written on it. Another car was parked beside it, so she couldn't see the full name, but pink flowers were part of the paintjob. That was what she saw on the video and that was what she needed to see now.

Chrys stopped the car for a moment to think about what to do. All she really needed to do was make sure that was the van. Then she could go to Wash. She changed gears and reversed back toward an empty parking spot. Parking in the front and walking around had to be less conspicuous.

Her foot hit the brake pedal.

Chrys flashed a crooked smile at the mother and two children, one of which nearly ran out behind the car. The mother snarled and shook her head as they all got into their own car with the tropical plants they just purchased.

Chrys' heart was now in her throat, so there was no problem hearing it pound. She had to calm down. This was just walking around and seeing if the van resembled the one from the video. After that she'd make a call.

She left empty dinner buns on the passenger seat as she got out of Jessie's car. Chrys wondered what was happening with Jessie. She was going with the rule that no news was good news. Of course how was she supposed to get any news? Again Chrys cursed that her phone was destroyed.

What was the plan? Find the van, find the psycho, call in the cavalry. Easy peasy. She wasn't sure how she was going to do step three without a phone, however.

Chrys tried to act as natural as she could until she was out of sight of the gift shop windows. She wasn't sure how to hold her hands. The moment she couldn't see the front windows she ran and planted her back next to the wall. She grit her teeth against the pain surging through her body. She checked behind her as a large truck went down the street. She couldn't see anyone, but that didn't mean she wasn't being watched. After all, O'Donnell had cameras, so why wouldn't someone else? She moved slowly. Her eyes were on the mini-van. She had to walk beside the greenhouse but there were no windows along the L shaped building. Could the people inside see her shadow through the foggy tarp covered wall? She couldn't see inside, so under the rules of hide-and-seek when she was a kid they couldn't see her.

"Chill out, girl," Chrys said out loud but to herself. "No need to freak out." She had to concentrate on her breathing. This was stupid. She had to get out of there. Her feet didn't stop moving forward. She wanted to run, but wanted to see if she was right as well. There were a lot of people that needed to know.

Each time her shoe went down the sound of sole on gravel seemed to echo along the building. All she could smell was dirt. It was one of those times you could smell the rain in the air. It was going to start falling soon. The farther she got from the gift shop the louder a generator got. It must have been what kept the heaters going inside.

She stepped around the car next to the mini-van. There they were. Her fingers ran across the pink flowers painted on the side of the van. This was the van from the video. If this was the killer's van how could it go unnoticed every time he took someone? Wouldn't they remember a van with flowers on it? Or would it just be another vehicle in a chaotic world? Maybe he was in the area enough that it just became part of the scenery. Spencer was face to face with the actual man and he couldn't remember what he looked like. Perhaps the van was the same. People remembered a clown because it was odd and different. A common face? A delivery van? Those things were just there.

"Hi."

Chrys saw the face. She saw the hand below the lips. The white dust in the air.

Oh God!

Chapter 37

Spencer's eyes searched the room as he stepped through the door to the tattoo studio across the street from his restaurant. A glass display case had nose rings, tongue rings, nipple rings and rings that he didn't want to know where they went. There was a price list for different piercings right next to a sign saying you had to be eighteen or older. The countertop was bright red and covered in stickers and decals from what he assumed were businesses having to do with tattoos and piercings. On the wall behind the counter (and behind plastic heads with different piercings and rings on them) were pictures of tattoos the artists had done. Chrys' shoulder tattoo was there. He glanced at the leather couches expecting to see her. The young woman behind the counter barely looked up at him and pointed to the back tattoo area.

"Hey Sloane, is Chrys at your place?"

Sloane was sorting through her inks. She looked up shaking her head. "No, she was knackered and wanted to go home. When I left her she was asleep. Everything alright?"

"Yeah, I haven't been over there yet. I called the apartment and there wasn't any answer, so I thought she might be with you. I'm sure she's sleeping."

"I'll go over with you," Sloane said as she closed the toolbox of inks and tattoo machine parts. As they walked through the door she asked how Jessie was.

Spencer stopped on the curb and watched a couple of cars drive by. "She's in recovery. They stopped the bleeding and fixed her up. Hanni stabbed her more in the shoulder than near vital organs, so she should be okay. We have to wait to see how much movement she'll have in her arm."

Customers were starting to show for dinner service. There was a few older people which had continued coming after Spencer bought the restaurant from his father. When they did come for a meal they came early.

As Spencer and Sloane walked through the front door to The Alcrest the scent of the grill touched their nostrils. The sounds of music, some conversation and the exhaust fan filled their ears. Sloane whispered "I'm going upstairs," before heading towards the back of the restaurant.

"Chef, how's Jessie?" Sue was behind the hostess stand. She was smiling but there was stress in her pretty face.

Every time Spencer looked at her he thought how the word pretty was a massive understatement. He didn't know how to describe her and found it uncomfortable to look at her. He quickly filled her in about Jessie's condition.

"What about Hanni?" Gordie pulled himself through the opening to the kitchen.

"She's okay too. The doctor doesn't think there'll be any side effects of the drug."

"Are you going to let her come back to work here?" Sue's voice shook. She brushed her hair back.

Gordie fixed the sleeve of his chef coat. "Yeah man, she tried to kill two of us."

"She was drugged with scopolamine. She did what she was told to do, it wasn't of her free will. That's the way this drug works. She won't even remember any of it." Spencer looked at the reservation book. There was none written down for tonight. All they might have is the couple tables of old farts that didn't order much to begin with. Perhaps closing on Sunday's, at least for the evenings would be a good thing. It wouldn't hurt the business much.

"Spencer," Sloane charged down the hallway, "Chrys isn't up there."

"What do you mean?"

"Yeah, Chrys left," Gordie said. It took a second before realizing they were waiting for him to say more. "What? She came down a few hours ago, went in the office for a few minutes then left."

"She took Jessie's car," Sue added.

"Where did she go?"

Gordie looked behind him as he was told they had a new order. "I don't know." He stepped into the line and looked over the order chit. "She said something about going to a flower shop or something. I didn't know she was under house arrest."

"She wasn't. She's just Chrys doing a Chrys move." Spencer bit his lip for a moment. "You said she went in the office?" He headed in that direction without an answer.

Why would Chrys go into his office and then leave? He saw her at the hospital where she couldn't move much. She was in pain and dead tired. Something had to get her up and moving. He stopped in the doorway to his office. Everything was in its place. If she came in here, then she didn't move anything. What was in his office that she wouldn't have to move?

Spencer crossed the room in two steps. The computer monitor was black. He touched the mouse waking it up. It wasn't his usual home screen. It was something else. The back parking lot of the restaurant was right there. He saw Jessie's car, his rental, other cars and the back steps. It was some type of video. He wanted to know where this came from, however that could wait. He clicked back on the video's timeline by a few minutes and pressed play.

"What is it?" Sloane had been silent on the other side of the desk.

Spencer clicked some more and stared at the screen. "Hanni's attack. There's a van." He motioned the tattoo woman to come to his side. She leaned over his shoulder. "Look, is that flowers on it? Maybe?"

"We have to call the police." Sloane looked from the monitor to the phone to Spencer. "Call that detective Chrys complained about. What's her name?"

Spencer stared at the screen. He had a good guess at where the video came from. The same guy who said he had taken steps to ensure their safety. He was keeping his eyes on them. "Wash. Detective Washburn. Chrys went to like, a half dozen flower places yesterday. This may not even be one of them and I don't know which one it is."

"The detective met us outside when we got back here and she talked to us. Chrys told her about a man at one place. Pacific Exotics."

Spencer got up quickly. "That's one I don't have to go to then."

"I'm going with you."

Spencer reached under the desk. The safe was there. Every night he or Jessie put the days take in there and every morning Spencer counted it a second time and deposited it in the bank down the street. He had changed how things were done shortly after last summer. He changed it so that he was the only one to put the money in and take it out. The moment he opened the safe he pulled out a box. He dialed the code into the tumblers on that and opened it too. His hand shook as he took hold of the 9mm pistol inside. It was heavy and cold, in more ways than one.

"You have to stay here."

"I'm not staying here." Sloane put her hand on the freezer so he'd have to go through her to get out.

Spencer pushed the clip of bullets into the gun with a loud click. "You have to stay here in case we don't come back." In that instant and with the look in his eyes Sloane's hand dropped.

Chapter 38

"I can't blame you. I'd like to blame you for finding me out and forcing me to come forward, but I can't really. Everything which has happened has been my fault." As I get to one side of the room I turn and pace back the other way. It smells of earth and dampness. It is different than outside however, this smell is stale as if the air never moves. "I could have gone on forever. Nobody even knew I was out there until I let them know. I did the same as Grandpa and got greedy. And you utilized that greed."

I have her in a chair at my small dining table. The drug took effect and she is my play thing. I step around behind her and run my fingers through her long hair. It's soft, silky. I watch her close to see if she flinches. Nothing. This one is different than all the others. She came to me. She found me. How far behind are the others? The lion could be circling at this very moment. She could have been the lamb put to slaughter. The bait. Or that stupid cop could be nearby. She knew nothing unless I told her.

"You were the smart one. All I wanted to do was make a statement. I wanted to have what my grandfather never had. Then I heard her scream."

Most of my belongings are packed in boxes. I'll leave and disappear back into the shadows where I have spent most of my life. And I'll kill again and again. I'll slaughter the useless waste, as Grandpa called them, by making them kill themselves. What depths can I have them take themselves to? I'll be nothing again. They'll look at me and not see a thing.

"It's not all about killing." I grab her breast and give it a squeeze. I can feel her heart beating through her clothes and skin. It beats fast like all the others. "I'm a weak man, Chrys. I don't want the women I can get on my own. I take things." I slip my hand inside her sweatshirt caressing her warm skin. I feel the growth in my pants. "I wanted your blond friend, but then you took from me, you took my grandfather's place, and I let anger take over my life. I had hopes she would kill you or the lion. As it was she didn't kill anyone, did she? And now you're here."

With finger and thumb I squeeze the nipple before pulling my hand out. I walk to the far side of the table. There are no plates or cutlery this time.

"She won't ever remember what she did, however she will always recall that she did it. I touched her too. Everyone else has, right? Your breasts are better." I don't often laugh, but can't help myself.

Behind me is a box of my tools and treasures. I have something from everyone. I even have Crystal's necklace back. On the top is my favorite toy. I walk back to where Chrys sits and place it gently on the table in front of her. Her brown eyes stare ahead.

"I'd love to play some more, but I really have to go. Take the saw handle." She moves slowly but her fingers find the handle of the hacksaw. I can't help but smile. "Put the blade on the elbow of your other arm and start sawing. Let's make a special wind-chime for the wolf." My eyes get wide as she does what I tell her. This is more exciting than having my hands on her. I can't wait to see the wolf's face. Will this wind-chime make him scream?

Chapter 39

Spencer looked in the rearview mirror. At the speed he was driving Middleton's finest was going to get on him soon enough. He swerved the rental car around a blue Ford going the speed limit. He looked at the GPS on his cellphone which sat on his right thigh. He had already driven by two of the greenhouses on Chrys' list. A bright yellow Volkswagen Beetle was hard to miss and he had yet to see it. The thought that Jessie's car could have been hidden kept creeping into his thoughts. And if he could hide that then he could hide Chrys. Searching every nook and cranny of every greenhouse and flower shop wasn't going to get him anything. He was already wasting too much time as it was.

"Where are you Chrys?"

The light ahead turned amber then red. His foot stomped on the brake pedal. The gun slid on the passenger seat. His phone said he was almost at the third greenhouse, Lonesome Dove Greenery. Odd name for a greenhouse. He remembered reading a book by that name a long time ago.

The light turned green.

Five minutes later he saw the bright yellow car he was looking for and he felt something leap in his chest. The greenhouse had a square building in the front. The sign above the door had the name with a picture of a white dove flying around colourful flowers. There was even a flower which looked like the ones Chrys had shown him near the edge of the sign. The ones that made scopolamine.

He parked beside Jessie's car and watched the front door through the rearview mirror. What would Chrys have done? He slipped the gun in his coat pocket. He'd have to keep his hand on it. From what Chrys said about scopolamine it worked fast with a blown kiss. He wasn't going to let anyone get close enough. As he stepped from the car he dialed a number with his right thumb as his left hand grabbed the grip of the gun in his coat pocket. It felt cold in his fingers. This foreign body. A chef knife was part of him, but this was a strange alien.

"Middleton City Police Department, how may I direct your call?"

He blinked three times. His sister was waiting for him. "Detective Washburn please. Homicide." It didn't sound like his voice. The lump in his throat was more than imaginary.

He could see a mini-van parked back where the building turned. If Chrys was here then that was the same van in the video clip. He didn't need to see it. All he needed to do was find his sister.

The front door opened.

Spencer's fingers flexed on the handle of the gun. He held his breath. His shoes skidded on the damp dirt.

A grey haired man walked through the doorway to the store. His faded shirt was tucked into his pants and a large shiny buckle fastened his belt. In his hands was a ceramic pot with dark leaves cascading over the sides. He never paid the chef any attention. He simply walked to his vehicle, buckled the plant in the back seat, got behind the steering wheel and drove away. Perhaps he just bought his wife or mother a birthday present. Go out to buy a plant and get shot by a nervous chef just for opening a door.

Spencer breathed. He hadn't even realized he was holding hi breath. His palms were already sweaty. He brought the phone back to his ear. Time to get on with this. For all he knew the psycho could have taken Chrys away. Bits and pieces of her could be hanging somewhere already.

"Detective Washburn, how can I help you?'

Her voice in his ear made him flinch again. "It's Spencer Alcrest."

"I was just visiting with your friend Jessie."

"Chrys wasn't home when I got there," Spencer ignored what the woman was saying. "I think she knows who he is or where he is and she's gone after him."

"What?" There was rustling and noise on her end like someone getting up quickly and knocking things over. "Spencer -"

"I'm here now. Her car is here. I'm going in to try and find her."

"No! Spencer, where are you? Give me a location and then stay outside." Her voice was frantic.

His was eerily calm. "I don't know how long she's been here, so I have to go in."

"Spencer, no. I can have officers wherever you are in fifteen minutes. Listen to me Spencer, do not go in wherever you are. Do not go in." You could tell through the phone line that she was moving.

"Lonesome Dove."

"What?"

Spencer turned the phone off and opened the front door with his fingers. Inside was an attack on the senses. There were items on every surface and hanging from walls and posts and even the ceiling. It was all artsy stuff. Conversation starters and focal points. He stopped for a moment to let his eyes search. The door leading to the greenhouse was directly across the room. An older man and woman were in one corner looking at stain-glass wind-chimes. The young woman behind the counter didn't pay him any attention. She was too busy on her phone.

The greenhouse was a totally different place. It was like walking through the door of the Tardis. The store was full and chaotic with music playing and air conditioning. You stepped through the door into another world. Tables ran along the outer walls and down the middle. All were covered with plants at different stages of growth and size. There were loud fans going to make sure the temperature stayed high inside the building. Sweat appeared from Spencer's pours immediately. This one long building went about thirty yards down then turned to another tube-like hallway. Spencer shut the door to the store and looked around. Chrys wasn't here, but under the drug she could be somewhere waiting. How long did Hanni wait to attack Jessie?

His fingers squeezed the gun handle as he stepped forward. He chose the right path. His shoes crunched on the earth floor. This was the part in the thriller movies where the hero carefully walked down the room toward the hiding killer. Spencer hated clichés.

"Anyone here? Hello?"

"Down here, Hun."

He heard the voice, but Spencer couldn't see the woman. The gun raised slightly, still hidden in the pocket. "Where are you?"

"Down here, I said." The woman stepped out from the other side long enough to wave at him and then stepped back. He saw denim, hair and boobs.

Spencer couldn't see her and he didn't like it. He kept himself on the far side of the path. It was hard to breathe in the humid greenhouse. He felt the panic sitting in his chest wanting to take hold.

"What can I help you with? We're having a sale on saplings; spruce, pine, balsam – domestic coniferous."

Spencer looked behind him then back to where she had popped out of. "I'm looking for my sister. She's Aboriginal, pretty, probably had a lot of bandages on her."

"Nope, can't recall anyone like that today." Her voice was flat with no concern at all.

"Her car is parked outside." Spencer reached where she was. The woman transferred plants to bigger pots and filled them with soil. She didn't wear gloves and had dirt deep in the creases of her fingers and under her fingernails. She had a lot of hair held up high on her head. She wore jeans and a half open shirt that screamed against her breasts. "You sure you didn't see her?"

"I can't be held responsible for people parking outside my building." With every move she made her large head of hair seemed to sit still. She put a trowel beside the pot she was working on. She continued her movements ignoring the fact that he was there. She had to be in her early fifties and by the lines on her face had experienced things.

Spencer was glad he was a leg man because he could have gotten distracted by her ample chest. The unicorn tattoo was humorous. As it was he didn't have the time and frustration was setting in. "She came by here yesterday. You sure you don't remember?"

The woman patted the dirt into the last pot, put it into place on a table, scraped the access dirt to the ground before walking past Spencer without a word and headed toward the corner of the greenhouse. "I have a lot of work to do. I have trees to prune. Do you know what it's like to run a business?"

Spencer struggled to keep up to her. "Don't you have workers? You have that girl out front."

"She just watches the store. I do everything in here and believe me it's a lot of work."

"Where are you going?"

"If you're a customer we can talk. Otherwise, I don't have time for your questions."

As they turned the corner in the L shaped building the small plants and flowers turned to bushes and small tropical trees. It even seemed hotter once the turn was made. Spencer was surprised there was such a market for tropical plants in Middleton. People wanted a piece of paradise he guessed.

"You have a guy working here for you, don't you?"

"No." She picked up a small set of sheers. A few more steps and she stopped to inspect a tree about her height. Stems hung over with bell like flowers.

"You sure?"

"It's my business. Of course I'm sure." Her voice raised.

Spencer didn't believe her. "He is average looking. So average you wouldn't even remember what he looked like after meeting him. Maybe he used to work here."

"I think it's time for you to leave, Hun." She pointed the sheers at him. He noticed how sharp they looked. "I don't know what you're talking about and I don't have time for this."

"Spencer."

He barely heard his name, but time stopped. He didn't hold his breath, he just couldn't breathe. He looked past the gardener and stared down the greenhouse. Twenty yards away Chrys stood inside an open doorway. The red on her body was amazingly bright. Blood had soaked into her clothes. There were splatters on her face and her right hand looked like she wore a red latex glove. Blood bubbled from a slice on the inside of her left elbow.

"Chrys?"

"I," she looked down at her hand. A drop of blood fell to the dirt on the floor. Everything was so silent they all heard it. Drip. As Chrys looked up her eyes were dark saucers. Her brother had never seen her skin so pale. "I think I killed him, Spence. I think …" She couldn't move.

"You couldn't have," The gardener took a few steps toward the bloody woman and stopped.

Chrys stared straight at them without seeing them. "He wanted me to cut my arm. I think I killed him."

"My son? You killed my son? No!" The sheers were raised. The woman screamed. She broke into a run.

Spencer blinked. This was crazy. What was happening?

Chrys stood still. She didn't even flinch when the two gunshots echoed in the greenhouse.

It wasn't until the woman dropped that Spencer felt the gun in his hand. He could smell the burnt gunpowder.

He dropped the gun beside his feet. He ran forward, jumping over the gardener who was strewn on the ground and in a few steps had his sister in his arms squeezing her close to his body. She didn't move her arms to embrace him, instead they hung limp at her sides. Drip. The blood transferred into his clothes. He didn't really care. He just wanted to hold his sister and make it alright.

He looked back over his shoulder. The woman wasn't moving. His cellphone started to ring.

"I killed him, Spencer." As he turned back to Chrys he found she was staring at him. He almost stepped back. "He thought he drugged me, but I had bread up my nose."

"What? Bread?"

"He touched me, but I stayed still. I killed him."

Spencer pulled her into him locking his arms around her. This time Chrys' arms circled him and squeezed him back. He was too slow in getting there. He heard Wash yelling his name and shortly after saw the police running down the greenhouse paths. All he could think was that he was too late.

Chapter 40

"I'll be right back," Spencer handed off the spatula to the closest person to him (Mallory quickly passed it off to Gordie) and jogged down the back stairs. With long strides he met the car which he saw coming down the street before it was halfway across the parking lot. He looked back over his shoulder at the top landing of the stairs. They had the barbeque going and everyone was moving in and out of the apartment.

"Spencer," Detective Washburn stepped out of the driver's seat of her silver Nissan 350z. Her hair was windblown from driving with the top down.

Spencer looked at her spiked heels before looking at her face. "How can I help you, Detective?"

"Wash or Zoe. I'm not on duty right now. It's been a few weeks, so I thought I'd come see how you're doing. What you did isn't easy for someone who's been trained to do it. I can't imagine what you've been going through."

"I'm okay." He smiled at her. He hoped she didn't see that he was lying to her. He wasn't okay. He had killed a woman by shooting her in the back. Whether she was going to kill Chrys or not was beside the point. He hugged his body and squeezed his arms close.

"If you ever need to talk, I've been there."

"I'm fine, really."

Wash looked up and stared at Chrys who had stepped up to the deck railing. She stared back with a blank expression on her face. "Has she told you yet what happened?

"I know the basics. She put balled up bread in her nostrils to block the scopolamine, but she didn't think about her eyes and mouth. She said she tripped out and the rest is … she hasn't told me a lot, no."

Wash' hands were in her jacket pockets. The wind picked up her loose hair and threw it on her shoulders. She pulled free a couple of strands which stuck to her lipstick. After Spencer was quiet for a while she said, "It takes time. She had to go over it with us, and I wish I could tell you what she said. All I can say is give her time. Maybe therapy." She reached out and gently squeezed his forearm. "I know when I first shot a suspect it took a huge toll on me. Therapy helped." She never removed her hand. "Drinking helped a lot too, but that brought its own problems."

He stared down at her fingers and the rings on them. "She's been going to my therapist that I started seeing after I was tortured. He helped me. Then and he's been helping me since this."

"Chrys was lucky you got there. We've been looking into the lives of the Ryder family. The two at the greenhouse were the daughter and grandson of Augustus Ryder. They basically had an apartment underneath the greenhouse and in there we found journals from both of them. She helped her father, when he killed people, trained her son. They had boxes of souvenirs from victims. A lot more than the thirty-five. You didn't tell me how you knew where Chrys was."

Spencer nodded before looking up where he thought O'Donnell's camera was. He couldn't see it. "It was all just a process of elimination."

Wash looked the direction he was gazing at and saw nothing. She dropped her hand. She looked at the landing and saw at least three people watching them. Chrys wasn't there anymore. "You're not opened today?"

Spencer shook his head. "We're closing on Sundays now. I have to save money somehow."

"How's Jessie?"

"Good, really good. She's upstairs. Since we're not working we're having a barbeque. You want to come up?"

"I have to go meet my husband. Some other time. How's Hanni doing?

Spencer shrugged. "Pretty much back to herself. She's just been working the busy nights."

"Is she here?"

"Not yet. She hasn't really been around Jess and Chrys that much. Can't blame her."

"Maybe it's for the best." Wash opened the driver door to her silver convertible and kept her hands on it. "She didn't seem to me to be in your league. I hope I'm not over stepping."

"It's all good. Who's in my league then? Older, married homicide detectives?" Spencer hadn't moved yet. The only thing that changed was that his smile had moved into his eyes and his cheeks, with their deep dimples, looked blushed.

Wash' face went red too. "I'm way, way out of your league. I'll see you around, Spencer Alcrest."

"You too, Detective Washburn."

~ * ~

"How are things going today, Chrys?"

Chrys didn't like looking directly at her therapist. Instead she stared at the dragon statue on his desk. "I'm afraid." It was one dragon body with two heads, each on their own long necks. They looked like they were in a fight with each other. Man's inner battle with himself.

"What are you afraid of?"

She looked to the side wall. There was a half dozen paintings hanging there. You could tell they were not made by a skilled hand. "Did you paint those?"

"No, my wife. She started going to those painting parties where they get taught a painting a night and drink wine. She's getting better, I think."

Chrys had been coming here since a few days after being at Lonesome Dove. She had already talked about how she didn't get the full effect of the drug and that she saw demons and pure evil when she was under. The images were real. She told him about the touching and that she was fully aware and didn't know when it was happening if she'd be able to do anything to stop him. When the psycho said to start cutting her arm she actually did. She felt the teeth tear at her skin. She saw her own blood run out. Then she swung. The hacksaw went into an arc slicing through his throat like there was nothing there. His blood splashed out. It hit her on the chest and face. Blood bubbled out and over his fingers desperately trying to stop the fountain gurgling out of his throat. He fell on her and more blood ran over her body. All she could do was sit there and watch him die. She told her therapist that on the first day. Since then she was avoiding anything having to do with that day.

"Did you tell Spencer what Liam O'Donnell told you about your real father?"

She shook her head. "I don't know how to tell him. How do you go, hey your dad cheated on your mom and we're actually blood related?"

"Is that what you're afraid of?"

Chrys shook her head. She moistened her lips. "This is all confidential, right?"

"You ask me that every time we meet. I can't tell anyone what you tell me. Especially not your brother."

She scratched the back of her hand even though it didn't itch. "I didn't tell you something about when the guy had me. When he was touching me I didn't hear his voice or see his face. I saw the guy who raped me when I was fourteen." She wiped tears off her cheeks. She looked up at the therapist for really the first time. She saw his green eyes and grey beard. She wanted to see his reaction. "And I liked killing him. I liked his blood on me and his life leaving his eyes. I liked it. It got me excited. Fuck, it got me horny."

"And that made you afraid?"

"What if I'm one of them?"

"I'm sure you have nothing to worry about, Chrys."

She stared right at him. She didn't state the extent that it excited her. She didn't have nightmares. She had erotic dreams about that night. About the blood. What if she wanted to kill? What if she craved it?

~ * ~

"You okay, Chrys?"

"Hmm?" She looked up at Spencer, her real brother. She sat in a living room lounger with Breeze in her lap, her fingers holding the Chihuahua's collar, staring off into nothing. Daydreaming. "I'm fine. What did Wash want?"

"Just to check in." He went down to one knee in front of her.

"How long is she going to keep checking in?"

"She's just making sure we're okay. Are you okay?"

"I will be. You and I are the city's heroes of the moment." She dropped her sarcastic tone when she saw the look in his eyes. "I'll survive, Spence."

"Stupid how they named the greenhouse after a book with a character with the same name, eh? Augustus McRae in Lonesome Dove. Maybe we should have realized that."

"They were a family of psycho's, Spence. I don't want to talk about it anymore."

Spencer squeezed her knee as he rose to his feet. "You want a burger?"

"Sure," how many secrets was she going to keep, "Big brother."

END

Well, what did you think? If you have any questions, comments or just want to say hi feel free to send me an email at lorneoliverauthor@gmail.com or visit my, to The Alcrest Mysteries pages on Facebook.

You never know, you could become a character like a fan named Samara who is going to be a character in the next Alcrest novel.

In the near future short stories, The Alcrest Stories, will be coming out. These will tell you about other crew members and all the crazy things they get into. If you really want to know what they are like and some behind the scenes info check out The Alcrest Gastropub Cookbook on most sites.

See you next time,
Lorne

Quick Beet Pickles

6	medium beets
	Coarse salt
1/3 C	cider vinegar
¼ t	freshly ground pepper
1/3 C	olive oil

Method

1. Place beets in a pot with cold water. Bring to a boil and add a couple teaspoons of salt. Reduce heat for a rolling boil.

2. Cook until they are tender (30 minutes or so), drain and let cool. Peel beets and slice into ¼ inch slices. Arrange on platter.

3. Whisk vinegar, 1 ¼ teaspoons salt and the pepper in a small bowl. Add the oil in a slow, steady stream, whisking until emulsified. Pour vinaigrette over beets and serve.

Baked Salmon and Salsa

4	Salmon portions
1 T	Cilantro, chopped
½ C	Butter, soft
2	English Cucumbers, deseeded and diced
6	Tomatoes, deseeded and diced
½	Red onion, diced
	Lime juice
	Cilantro, chopped
	Salt and Pepper

Method

1. Put cucumber, tomato, onion together in a bowl. Add in enough lime juice and cilantro with adjusts to your taste. Season with salt and pepper. Set aside.

2. Mix cilantro into the softened butter.

3. Put a pan on the stove to medium-high heat. Add a touch of canola oil with a little of the cilantro butter. Place salmon into pan, skin side down. Cook for a few minutes to crisp skin. Remove pan from heat, add a dollop of cilantro butter onto each salmon and place in a preheated 350 degree oven for approximately 15 minutes.

4. Serve with salsa on top.